A MEMORY TO CHERISH

KAY CORRELL

ROSE QUARTZ PRESS

Published by Rose Quartz Press

ISBN 978-1-944761-25-7

021119

Memories dance in and out of the light... cherish them while you can.

This book is dedicated to each and every person taking care of someone with Alzheimer's disease. May you find strength, courage, and patience.

Find more information on all my books at
kaycorrell.com

COMFORT CROSSING ~ THE SERIES

The Shop on Main - Book One
The Memory Box - Book Two
The Christmas Cottage - A Holiday Novella
(Book 2.5)
The Letter - Book Three
The Christmas Scarf - A Holiday Novella
(Book 3.5)
The Magnolia Cafe - Book Four
The Unexpected Wedding - Book Five

The Wedding in the Grove - (a crossover short

story between series - with Josephine and Paul from The Letter.)

LIGHTHOUSE POINT ~ THE SERIES
Wish Upon a Shell - Book One
Wedding on the Beach - Book Two
Love at the Lighthouse - Book Three
Cottage near the Point - Book Four
Return to the Island - Book Five

SWEET RIVER ~ THE SERIES
A Dream to Believe in - Book One
A Memory to Cherish - Book Two
A Song to Remember - Book Three

INDIGO BAY ~ A multi-author sweet romance series
Sweet Sunrise - Book Three
Sweet Holiday Memories - A short holiday story
Sweet Starlight - Book Nine

Sign up for my newsletter at my website *kaycorrell.com* to make sure you don't miss any new releases or sales.

CHAPTER 1

Beth screamed.

The tapping at the car window started again.

"Lady, you need help?"

The rain poured down, obstructing any clear view of the man. Yes, she needed help. No, she wasn't going to open her car door to an absolute stranger while stuck out in the middle of nowhere. That's the stuff that always started segments of those Unsolved Mystery shows.

"It's Mac McKenna. I live in that town you just passed a few miles back."

Mac McKenna? Opening the car door to him might be more dangerous than inviting a complete stranger to rescue her. But she did need help, and she needed it quickly.

She rolled the window down slightly to get a look at him.

Mac McKenna in the flesh. And very well put together flesh if she remembered correctly.

"I have a flat," she said, as though he weren't standing practically next to the deflated front driver's side tire.

"Need help changing it?"

"No, I'm quite capable of changing it myself, but it's pouring down rain, and I'm late for an important meeting." She sounded like a pompous jerk. He probably thought she *was* one.

She peered out through the pouring rain, scrutinizing what she could see of him not hidden by his cowboy hat and his rain slicker, which wasn't much.

"I could give you a lift." His crooked smile suggested he knew she was giving him the once over.

Accept a ride from him? What, did she look crazy? Of course, her options were slim to none. If she missed the meeting, her chances of making a good impression at the town council meeting were going to be washed away with the rain.

She'd go with him. With any luck, not a soul would see them.

"Okay. Thanks for the offer. I need to get to Watson Elementary School."

He delayed an almost imperceptible moment in answering. "Sure, no problem." He tipped his well-worn cowboy hat farther back on his head to keep the rain from dripping down on her as he swung open her door.

Beth grabbed the box resting beside her and piled her purse and some books on top of it. She tried to maneuver out while balancing the box.

"Here, let me get that." He confiscated the box, tucked it under one arm, and reached out a hand to help her.

She ignored the hand and quickly slid out of the car, carefully locking the door behind her. He spread his rain slicker out to the side and tucked her close under his arm. Safe. Dry. She couldn't squirm away without being obvious… and wet.

He led the way to an old red pick-up truck parked behind her car, opened the passenger side door, and she slipped inside. He unceremoniously dumped the box on her lap and closed the door.

The inside of the truck was meticulously clean. Worn leather seats, cleaned and polished. Dashboard clear of the bits of paper, receipts, and pens that cluttered her own car.

"Oh, wait," she said.

He paused as he started to haul himself in on his side. "What's wrong?"

"I have one more file in the trunk that I need." The file had facts and figures she'd painstakingly put together for tonight's meeting. She couldn't show up without them.

He reached out his hand while she used every ounce of her concentration to keep from shrinking away from it. "Give me your keys. I'll get it."

"That's okay. I'll get it."

"In case you've forgotten, it's raining out here. Just give me the keys. I'll be right back."

She handed him the keys. "It's on top of a stack of stuff on the left side of the trunk."

She squinted, trying to watch through the window. She saw him dash through the rain, open the trunk, grab the file, and hurry back. He climbed in, pushed the file at her, then coaxed the truck to life. He pulled the truck onto the road and concentrated on driving through the pouring rain. The radio played country music quietly in the background. He nodded his head at her. "Seatbelt."

"What? Oh, sure." She grabbed the belt and buckled up.

The wipers swished back and forth, trying their best to clear the window. She didn't know how he could even see the road, and this wasn't a mountain road to mess with. Knowing the luck she was having today, she'd end up in the ditch with him out here in the middle of nowhere, no better off than she'd been back there with her flat. Well, actually, quite a bit worse off.

Mac McKenna.

Just what she needed right now, another complication.

He drove on in silence. Not a word since the admonishment to buckle up. The air in the truck crackled with tension. Was it just the strain of driving in the torrential rain, or was he upset with her? She hadn't meant to jerk away from his offered hand when getting out of her car. But all her instincts were in overdrive. This was Mac McKenna. Trouble. With a capital T.

She'd been a few years behind him in school, but his reputation was legend. The same school district that now employed her. The school where the town council meeting was being held tonight in the gymnasium. That school.

She turned toward him in the cab of the truck. She hadn't even told him her name. Maybe it was safer that way. An anonymous face. No, she was being paranoid. "I don't know where my manners have gone. I haven't even introduced myself. I'm Beth Cassidy."

"Yeah, I know."

"You do?" Did he remember her?

No, he couldn't.

But he supplied no further information. Instead, he stared out the window, squinting in an effort to see through the shower of rain descending on the windshield.

He stole a quick glance at her. "After I drop you off, I'll go back and fix your flat."

"No thanks, Mr. McKenna. I'll get someone to drop me back off by the car.

"Mac."

"What?"

"Mac. Just Mac. Not Mr. McKenna. And suit yourself on the car. I was just trying to help."

"Thanks anyway… Mac. I'll take care of it after the meeting. I do know how to change a

tire. I just don't want to be late to this meeting."
Or show up bedraggled in sopping wet, muddy
clothes. She needed to look organized, efficient,
and competent.

Then the hail started, bouncing off the roof
of the truck and sounding like God was pouring
down buckets of stones on them. Mac pulled
the vehicle off the side of the road at a small
turnoff that she knew overlooked the town of
Sweet River Falls. It also had a steep drop-off.
She hoped *he* knew that. She caught her breath
as the truck rolled to a stop near the edge.

He seemed oblivious to her angst. "Can
hardly see anything. Let's give it a few minutes
to let up."

She glanced at her watch but realized there
was nothing else they could do. It was suicidal to
drive on these mountain roads in this storm.
Hopefully, it would let up soon. She had to get
to that meeting. For the hundredth time, she
berated herself for taking the shortcut home
from Denver. She had wanted the grant forms
signed and didn't want to wait for them to be
mailed. She wanted them in her hands, signed,
so she could... Well, so she could show them off
at the meeting. Prove that she always had the
town's best interest at heart.

She'd rushed off to the city and took this supposed shortcut back home. So if she was late to the meeting, it was all her fault. Just one more poor decision in a series of bad decisions she seemed to be making these days.

Mac turned off the engine and lounged back in the seat. How could he look so relaxed? She reached up and rubbed her temples. The pounding hail reverberated in every muscle, every fiber.

"How can you just sit there and ignore the noise?" She had to practically shout to get him to hear her.

"Nothing we can do about it." His words echoed clearly in the truck even though she was sure he hadn't increased his volume one bit. His voice was deep, reassuring, and practical, which, truth be told, kind of annoyed her.

She leaned back in the seat too. Next thing she knew, he'd scooped the box off of her lap and dumped it into the space behind the seat. "Might as well get comfortable." He shrugged out of his rain slicker and dropped it behind the seat as well.

"I'm going to be late."

"So will everyone else. It's not just raining on us you know."

She glared at him. "Thank you, Mr. Weatherman."

"Look, lady. I'm just trying to get you to your meeting. It's not my fault you had a flat. I didn't make it rain." His eyes reflected amusement, not irritation.

She sighed. "I know. It's just that this meeting is——"

"I know. I heard. Important."

"Well, it is." How could he understand her very future may depend on this meeting? Not to mention the future of her mother and a good number of the people in the town. She sounded melodramatic, even to herself, but the meeting *was* important.

He nodded but didn't look like he believed the meeting was life or death. The cad then settled back and watched the rain. The windows fogged over and gave the inside of the truck a feeling of being shut off from the world.

It was kind of cozy.

It was kind of *scary*.

She was stuck in the middle of nowhere. With a certifiable troublemaker. One who she hadn't been able to get out her mind in all the years since high school. Well, maybe she was the one who was certifiable.

Certifiably crazy.

No one thought about *one* incident, one teeny tiny encounter with him, that happened all those years ago. He probably didn't even remember it. Or if he did, he probably didn't remember it had been her. Why had that one incident from high school stuck in the recesses of her memory for all this time?

She chanced a quick glance over at him. The years had given a hard edge to the planes of his face. His tanned face gave him the look of a man who liked to be outdoors. Dark black hair curled slightly at the collar of his denim shirt. Just a tad too long to be stylish.

She quickly turned away before he could catch her staring at him.

MAC GLANCED OVER AT BETH. Her honey-brown hair was still long, but not as long as it had been in high school. Today she wore it pulled back in some kind of fancy braid. He watched her fidget uncomfortably in the seat and glance at her watch for about the hundredth time. He'd like to snatch that watch off her wrist and pitch it out the window.

"Why don't you just relax? There's nothing you can do about the storm."

She sighed and rolled her shoulders forward and back. "I know. I'm just frustrated."

Frustrated? He knew what frustrated meant. Trapped in this truck with her, after all these years. He swiped at the fogged over windows, but it didn't help. He still couldn't see a thing, and it didn't relieve the tension hammering through him. She wasn't two feet from him. Her skirt was draped casually across her lap, wrapped around the outline of slim, shapely legs. She chewed nervously on her lower lip.

He was sure she didn't even remember him. No, correction… she seemed to remember his *reputation*. He'd seen the instant recognition in her eyes when he'd said his name. She'd looked like she was walking into the lion's den when she'd climbed in his truck.

She wiped at a runaway drop of rain that rolled off her damp hair. She reached up to the visor and flipped it down.

He smothered a grin. "Sorry, no mirror." She didn't really think he was the lighted vanity mirror type, did she?

"Oh. Well, I just thought I might be able to

repair some of the damage before I drag into the meeting looking like a drowned rat."

Lady, you don't look anything like a drowned rat. He watched her open her purse and drag out assorted makeup and a tiny mirror. He flipped on the overhead light in the cab of the truck.

"Thanks."

He watched in fascination as she touched here and there on her face with a smattering of pads and wands. When she was finished, she'd removed all trace of rain damage, but he'd be hard-pressed to tell she had any makeup on, except for a trace of lipstick, nearly the color of lips.

She must have felt his stare. She looked over at him and with obvious, sudden self-consciousness dumped the makeup back in her handbag. Then looked at her watch again. That very same watch he'd wished would die a sudden death. Maybe he could toss it onto the road and roll over it with his truck...

And why was his side of the truck fogged over so much more than her side? He shifted uncomfortably in the seat.

"So you said you own a restaurant?" Beth looked over at him with the warmest brown eyes he'd ever seen. No, he'd seen those same eyes before, in the face of a young, innocent, very surprised girl.

But he knew he hadn't said one word about what he did. "No. I own a tavern."

"Oh, I thought I'd heard it served sandwiches and burgers…"

"We do. But it's still just a tavern, a bar. People come to drink. To visit. To hang out. And they sometimes get hungry." So she'd heard about his business. Undoubtedly it fit in perfectly with her recollection of his reputation.

She shifted in her seat, and her skirt clung tightly to her left leg, but he ignored it. Kind of.

Stop it, Mac. Get a grip.

"And what do you do, Miss Cassidy?" He knew darn well what she did, but conversation seemed like a safe way to spend the time. That or ogle her like some love-starved high school kid.

"I'm a teacher at Watson Elementary School. I teach third grade."

"And the meeting you're in such a hurry to get to?"

"Town council meeting. It's a meet the candidates meeting." She chewed her bottom lip. "I'm… well, I'm running for mayor."

He choked back his surprise. Now that was

one thing he hadn't expected to hear. Beth Cassidy for mayor? Sweet River Falls seemed much more like the good-old-boy, slap-you-on-the-back mayor town.

"Hm, so probably not the best meeting to miss."

She shot him a deadly look. "I'm not going to miss this one. I can't. They'll think…" She cut herself off and turned to look out her window.

He almost told her she wasn't going to be able to actually *see* anything through the wind-lashed rain. "They'll think what?"

She turned and looked at him with those eyes framed in long, curling lashes. "I'm running against James Weaver. He has powerful friends in this town. The town has never had a woman mayor—it's not the most, um, progressive town around. The people that might consider voting for me are a bit leery of considering a woman for the job, and if they think a little rainstorm can keep me from a meeting, my credibility will drop about a zillion points."

He knew about the closed minds of some of the people in town all right. He was surprised they were even considering her for the job. Well, of course legally they had to. But saying the leaders of this town weren't the most progressive was like saying his homemade chili was a *little* spicy.

"Even men get flat tires," he said dryly.

"Of course they do." She bristled. "But I refuse to look like a helpless woman." She banged her fist on the dashboard and let out a mild curse word almost silently under her breath.

"Nice language."

"What? Only men can swear?"

Her eyes flashed with fire, and he had to keep from smiling at the sight. She sure was an easy one to rile. He was glad to see the windows on her side of the truck were fogging over now too. "I try not to swear in the presence of ladies."

"Thanks so much for the kind consideration."

Two swaths of red highlighted her checks. He thought she might actually be embarrassed to be caught swearing. He grinned at her.

"What are you smiling about? There's nothing funny here. I have to get to that meeting."

"Okay. Let's give it a shot. The rain is letting up some." He needed to get out of here. Out of the closed space. With her leg so near he could touch it without hardly moving. With the scent of flowers drifting around him. He faintly remembered that scent. Surely she didn't still wear the same perfume?

He flipped the key and the truck ground to life. He heard her let out a sigh.

Yeah, honey. Let's get out of here. Fast.

THEY COULDN'T GET out of there fast enough for Beth. How was it possible the front seat had become so small as they waited for the rain to lessen? She was sure he hadn't been this close to her when they started out.

She squished herself farther to her side of the seat. She wondered if it was some kind of sign that she ran into Mac McKenna today, of all days. She peered out the window as they hit the streets of town. Surely no one could see her in here with all the rain. Just what she needed to make a smashing impression. Show up at the town council meeting with the biggest troublemaker the school had ever seen. Old Mr. Dobbs had been a teacher back when Mac was out breaking every rule the school had ever made. Long retired from teaching, he now presided over the council with a closed-minded, iron fist.

They pulled up to the front door of the school. She intended to grab the box and run before anyone saw her.

"Here, I'll get the box." Mac reached behind the seat and hefted the box onto his lap. "I'll carry it in for you."

"No, I'll get it." She knew her words came out too fast. Too obvious.

He looked at her for a moment, steel eyes hardening. "No, I insist." He slid out of the truck and was opening her door before she had any time to protest any further.

She climbed out, glancing around to see if anyone was in the parking lot. When they got in the front door, she turned to him. "Here, I can take it now. Thanks for your help."

He moved the box from her reach. "I'll get it. No problem."

"Don't be silly. I'm perfectly able to carry the box."

"And I'm perfectly able to carry it, too, and escort you safely to your meeting."

"I don't need an escort." She glared at him.

Mr. Dobbs chose that exact moment to walk

17

through the front door. He stopped dead in his tracks and stared at Mac. Then at Beth.

"Miss Cassidy. I see you made it. I wasn't sure if this storm would keep some people safely at home." He looked closely at Mac. "Mr. McKenna, haven't seen you around these parts since… well, in quite a while." Old Man Dobbs left no doubt that he recognized the renowned troublemaker.

Mac's hand encircled her elbow. She couldn't just jerk away and make a fool of herself. "Here, hon. Let's get your things into the meeting." His deep, clear voice said each word slowly and distinctly.

Dobbs about had a heart attack on the spot. She turned and glared at Mac. More than a glare. A look that would tell him he could drop from a heart attack right along with Old Man Dobbs. Mac grinned back at her with an exaggerated innocent look plastered on his face.

The three of them walked to the gymnasium, unfortunately, all in perfect health.

CHAPTER 2

The voices in the cafeteria drifted into the distance as Mac strode away. Away from the stares. Away from the look in Beth's eyes. She'd been upset to be seen with him. He'd seen it clearly register across her face. He couldn't blame her. She was running for mayor and walked in with the biggest troublemaker the school and possibly the town had ever laid eyes on. He'd always be an outcast here. A loser. A never-do-well. A weirdo. An outsider. He could hear the litany of name calling that he'd endured his entire school life.

The feelings he'd worked so hard to bury deep in his subconscious struggled to the surface. He struggled right back until he reached the door of the cafeteria, then he lost the battle.

He took a deep breath as the familiar smells of the school washed over him. It still smelled faintly of disinfectant and spoiled milk. He hadn't been in there since the day he graduated from grade school, and when he thought about it, he didn't particularly have the desire to be here now.

The past came back like a wave of nausea. Same round tables with gray-white Formica tops. The table where he'd always sat.

In the corner.

By himself.

Choosing the chair that placed his back to most of the cafeteria. Squaring his shoulders in a nonchalant pose while he ate his lunch from a battered brown bag.

The kids would come by and kick the chair legs or bump into the back to try to make him spill his drink. He always carefully ignored them.

An invisible hand tightened around his heart as he remembered those miserable days. Then there had been the weeks the sixth-grade boys had let him sit with them. He'd started a fire in the trash can in the boys' bathroom, and they'd been impressed. Strange the things that impressed kids that age. They told him he could sit with them as long as he did a prank they'd dream up for him to do each week. And he had, so desperate to fit in somewhere.

He'd written cuss words on the bathroom walls, taken a key and scratched the principal's car, and run a pirate flag up the flagpole. He couldn't even remember all the things they told him to do. But he could remember the feeling of dread each Monday morning, wondering what they were going to have him to do that week.

Then they'd told him to slash the tires on Miss Henderson's car. The only teacher who had treated him like he was important. The only teacher who had always patiently answered his questions and didn't treat him like a dummy. He remembered the day clearly. It was pouring down an icy rain. The wind whipped sheets of water across the parking lot. He hadn't been able to do it. Miss Henderson would have come out to her car after dark. She was always staying late. She would have had to either call someone to change it or get soaked changing it herself, if she even knew how. He couldn't do that to her.

He'd promptly gotten bumped back to his

solo table, enduring the jeers and remarks about the dummy table, eating his lunch as quickly as possible so he could escape out to the edge of the playground until it was time to go back to class.

Mac shook his head, clearing the memories that floated past his vision. He turned his back on the cafeteria, on the past, and hurried out of the school, letting the front door slam behind him.

"THANKS, Sophie. I really appreciate the lift." Beth gathered her papers from the presentation she'd given at the meeting and stashed them in the box. "I know it's out of the way for you."

"It's really no problem. It's not like I have a hot date tonight or anything." Sophie grabbed a stack of papers and helped stuff them in the box. "Besides, you knew I'd come to the meeting tonight in support of you. You did a great job. I think people were impressed that you filed for the grant money to help fund the library technology expansion."

"I don't know if they were impressed, but it's needed funds. We need to get more computer access for the people who can't get a good internet signal way out in the mountains. The library seems like the logical place." Beth looked around to make sure she hadn't forgotten anything.

"I think you're right. There are those few computers that Annie put in her new addition to Bookish Cafe, and she has free wireless internet for people to bring laptops, but more access at the library is needed. I also like how the grant would include more funds for the library to purchase ebooks. You did a great job on this."

"If we get the grant."

"At least you're out there trying. Which is more than James Weaver is doing. He's just running around shaking hands all over town." Sophie slipped on her coat.

Beth gave the area one last look around to make sure everything was picked up and ready for tomorrow's school day. "At least it stopped raining. I should be able to get the flat fixed and home before long."

"I wish you'd just wait for the garage to fix it."

"They said they couldn't get to it until tomorrow. I need the car first thing in the morning." She shrugged as they walked out of the school. "Besides, I know how to change a tire. I have my gym bag in the car. I'll slip on my sweats and tennis shoes and have it changed in no time."

Sophie pushed the door open with one hip. "Well, as long as my old clunker makes it out to where you left your car, we should be set."

They hurried to her friend's car. Car was such a generous name for the vehicle. An old yellow Volkswagen bug that she nursed along from year to year. Sophie had had it since they were both in high school, but she loved the rattletrap and refused to part with it.

They climbed in and headed out to the west edge of town. Sophie fidgeted restlessly until she finally blurted out, "Whatever made you show up with Mac McKenna?" She glanced over at Beth.

"Oh, don't beat around the bush, please." She smiled at the woman seated next to her. They'd been friends since kindergarten. Sophie never was one for keeping her opinions to herself. "I didn't really have a choice. I needed a ride. He was there." She shook her head. "I didn't think he'd make such a big deal and walk me inside. I'm sure the council will have a field day talking about it."

Sophie gave her a supportive smile. "I'm sure they'll find something new to gossip about within the week. Just you wait and see."

Beth rubbed the back of her neck and rolled her shoulders. "I hope so. The last thing I need right now is a bunch of rumors flying around. Beth Cassidy and Mac McKenna, of all people."

She was aware he'd deliberately escorted her inside. He'd noticed her discomfort and taken advantage of it.

Or… *shoot*, maybe she'd hurt his feelings. She felt like a jerk.

This was too complicated to think about now. She was dead tired. She scrubbed her hands over her face and tucked a wayward lock of hair behind her ear.

"Your presentation went well." Sophie interrupted her thoughts. "All the things you have planned to help the town. The grant for the library that you already applied for. Maybe if you get the mayor job things will start to change around here."

"That's a big maybe. First, I would have to win the election. Win against James Weaver. And since he's a man, I'm *sure* he's better qualified. Just ask Dobbs."

Sophie grinned. "Yeah, a man must be more qualified than a mere woman. Even if he's the most non-progressive man ever. He'll keep the town firmly entrenched in the last century if they hire him."

"But he never rocks the boat. And I have a habit of always seeing how hard I can rock it without actually tipping it over."

"One of these days, you're going to go splashing into the water."

"Don't I know it." She shrugged. "I just keep pushing and prodding. Sooner or later, they have to move into this century. I have to be careful not to push too hard though. I can't afford to alienate people if I want them to vote for me. I have to convince them that my ideas are good for the town."

"Well, Weaver is buddies with Dobbs, so he'll do everything Old Man Dobbs wants him to."

"And if James is elected, he'll get a say on the planning commission, and if Dobbs gets his way, there's a good chance he'll ruin Lone Elk Lake by allowing high-rise condominiums to be built on it. But Dobbs only cares that it will put money in his own pocket. He doesn't care about things that will actually benefit the town."

"You mean things that benefit the town like the river walk that your mother and Annie championed? Or the grant for technology for the library?" Sophie rolled her eyes.

Beth grinned back at her friend. "Yes, things like that. I kind of really push when I believe in something."

"Gosh, I wonder where you got that stick-to-your plans trait from? Not your mom, I'm sure."

"I might have picked up a bit of her persistency character trait." Beth sighed. "Well, I'm sure that Dobbs favors a man for mayor. He hasn't quite heard of equal rights yet."

She looked over at her friend. What would she do without Sophie? Always there for her. Listening to any and every problem she ever had. Standing firmly by her side when her husband—ex-husband—had left her for the blonde bombshell who was just two years past being crowned homecoming queen. He must be fifteen years older than, what's her name... Bambi or something.

"Slow down." Beth pointed out the window. "There's my car."

Sophie pulled off the edge of the road. "I'll stay until the tire is fixed."

Beth dug in her purse for her keys. "Hey,

turn on the overhead light. I can't find my keys in this mess of a purse."

Sophie flipped on the light. "Find them?"

She dumped the contents of the purse on the seat and dug through the mess. She checked the pockets of the purse. Nothing. She sighed and looked up at Sophie. "I don't have them."

"What do you mean, you don't have them? You lost them?"

"No, I gave them to Mac McKenna to get a file out of my trunk. I must not have gotten them back."

"You sure?"

"Positive."

"Well, I guess it's on to Mr. McKenna's for your keys. Do you know where he lives?"

"He owns Mac's Place in Mountain Grove. We could try there. Could you drive me out to his bar? I'm sorry. I know this is out of your way." Beth shoved her hair out of her face, aggravated that she hadn't thought to rescue the keys from Mac after he retrieved the files for her. So much for his gallantry. It had only caused her to have to traipse over to Mountain Grove.

She immediately felt embarrassed about how ungrateful she sounded, even if it was only in her thoughts. Men didn't usually throw her so off-kilter like Mac McKenna did.

"On to Mountain Grove. Like I said, no hot prospects tonight anyway." Sophie grinned, then pulled back onto the road. "I'd kind of like to see you meet up with Mac McKenna again anyway."

SOPHIE PULLED into the parking lot of the bar. A neon sign in the window flickered brightly, proclaiming they were open. A lighted sign over the door said simply Mac's Place. The lot was full of pickup trucks of every size and variety. Old ones. New ones with extended cabs. A bright yellow one with a flame painted down its side.

"I've never seen so many trucks in my life." Beth stared at them.

"Looks like this is the place to be around here. Let's go in and see the infamous Mac McKenna. I was sorry I didn't get to the meeting early enough tonight to see you waltz in on his arm." She switched off the car and gathered up her purse.

"I did *not* waltz in on his arm." Beth shoved open the door to the car to emphasize her point.

"Whatever you say." Sophie didn't sound convinced.

They headed across the gravel parking lot, carefully avoiding the numerous puddles from the recent rain. Sophie pulled open the big wooden door and they crossed into the tavern. Beth blinked, giving herself a moment to let her eyes adjust to the dim lighting. As her eyes adjusted she noted everyone in the place was staring at them. She straightened her shoulders and zigzagged through the tables to the long wooden bar, ignoring the inquiring expressions of the patrons she passed.

"I'm looking for Mac McKenna," she said to the man tending the bar.

He looked at her for a moment. He looked at Sophie. She wasn't sure he was going to answer her. Then he nodded his head in the direction of a doorway beside the bar. "Back there."

Beth grabbed at Sophie's sleeve and tugged her toward the doorway. She didn't have a chance to go any farther. Mac came pushing through the swinging door with a gray plastic tub of ice balanced on one hip and a cartoon of beer bottles on the other hip.

Mac glanced up and stopped in his tracks. The man behind the bar sauntered over and took the tub of ice. "These ladies are looking for you, Mac."

"I see that. Miss Cassidy." He nodded at Beth. "Ma'am." He nodded Sophie. "What can I do for you?"

Beth just stood there for a moment, then felt Sophie's finger jab her side. "Oh. Well. I mean. I think you have my car keys."

"I do?"

"From when you went and got the file out of the trunk for me. You never gave them back."

"Hm, they must be in my rain slicker. I'm sorry you had to come chasing after them."

"No, *I'm* sorry. You're the one who rescued me and drove me into town in time for the meeting. I should be thanking you."

"Okay, now that you're both sorry, can we find the keys?" Sophie interrupted with an amused look on her face.

"My slicker is hung in the back room. Let me go check." He disappeared through the swinging door.

"Hey, you didn't tell me that Mac McKenna

31

the troublemaker turned into Mac McKenna the hunk." Sophie's voice was a loud whisper.

"Sophie!" Beth looked around to make sure no one had heard.

"What? Tell me you didn't see how he filled out those jeans. And that t-shirt. Gorgeous."

"Sh! Someone will hear you." Beth grabbed Sophie's sleeve again and tried to pull her farther away from the people sitting at the bar, but not before seeing the amused expression on the face of the man behind the wooden counter.

Mac pushed through the door again. "Here they are. I'm sorry."

"Let's not start in on the sorrys again." Sophie held out her hand to Mac. "Here, I'll introduce myself. Sophie Brooks."

Beth sent her a withering look, only Sophie just grinned.

"Miss Brooks."

"I gave Beth a ride so she could change her tire. Found out she didn't have her keys. Came here. Went through the I'm sorry routine. And there you have it."

Mac grinned at her. "Mac." He shook her hand. "Pleased to meet you."

"We actually went to school together. I was a

few years behind you. I knew who you were though. Quite a reputation."

"One I've not been able to live down, it appears, if you still remember me." He flashed her a wry grin.

"It looks like you've turned out just fine." Sophie grinned right back at him. Beth shot her a be-quiet-right-now look. And while the two of them were at it… they could quit grinning at each other.

"How about I follow you ladies back to the car and help change the tire…" He held up one hand. "I know, I know, you know how to change a tire. I'd like to help, though."

"You know, that would be great." Sophie jumped in before Beth had a chance to refuse. "I can't change a tire to save my life. No desire to, I guess. I call the auto club. As matter of fact, if you're going to help Beth, if you don't mind, I'll just head back to town. I have to meet someone later anyway."

Beth looked at her friend in desperation. What was she thinking? The liar. She did *not* have a date. "Sophie, we can't put Mr. McKenna out like that. Just drop me off at my car and you head on back to town. I'll be fine." She pinched her friend's arm.

Sophie rubbed her arm and smiled. "I couldn't leave you alone out there."

"No, you couldn't." Mac nodded gravely. "I'll take her back to her car and stay until the tire is fixed."

Beth looked helplessly back and forth between the two people who were now controlling her life. "Fine. Whatever works for you two, by all means." She could swear that Mac was offering to help because he could see it made her uncomfortable. And she knew very well that Sophie was dodging away in one of her numerous attempts to fix up Beth.

With Mac McKenna of all people.

What other surprises did this day hold in store for her?

CHAPTER 3

The night had cooled off considerably, and the wind picked up as they were leaving Mac's Place. Sophie headed off in her Volkswagen that bucked with a syncopated beat before rumbling out of the parking lot. She waved as she pulled away.

Traitor.

Mac led the way around back to where his truck was parked.

He held the door open for her while she climbed in. Trucks were high off the ground. Really high. Must be made for tall men. She ungracefully scrambled inside.

Beth snapped her seat belt and sat there while he crossed in front of the truck and swung up into the cab. No problem. The height of the truck sure didn't bother him.

They rode in silence. She wasn't sure what to say to this man. She caught herself just before she could have another uncharitable thought about it being dark out so no one would see her riding with him. Again.

Since when did she care so much what people thought?

Since she decided to run for mayor.

Appearances may be important right now, while she was running for mayor, but embarrassment washed through her. She wasn't an unkind person. Mac had been nothing but helpful to her all day. For goodness' sake, he was being *kind* to her.

His reputation as a troublemaker might have followed him all these years… just like Sophie was known as the big-hearted, do-anything-for-you person to go to in times of trouble. Old Man Dobbs was known to be set so far in his ways that he couldn't see the forest for the trees. Gloria Edmunds was known as the one who knew everything about everyone in town and spread rumors like a champion. The town stuck a label on you and it stayed there forever. Beth knew her label—the girl who got dumped by the high school football quarterback. Never mind that the dumping came after ten years of marriage after they were already out of college.

Obviously, Mac could have changed. She just didn't know this grown-up Mac McKenna well enough to judge. She settled back against the seat and watched out the window. The headlights pierced like a sword of light, parting the foggy night and illuminating the center line. It was mesmerizing in a haunting kind of way. Tucked safely in the truck. The only two people for miles around.

She stole a glance at him as he concentrated on the driving. The lines of his face were relaxed now. He didn't look nearly as threatening as he had this afternoon.

"You finished staring at me?" He glanced over at her.

She fought off the heat of a rising blush. "I wasn't staring. Just thinking."

"About what?"

"About—" She caught herself right before she blurted out she was thinking about him. "Things. I was just thinking about things."

"Things?"

"You know, you'd get along great with Sophie. She asks a lot of questions, too." As soon as the sentence was out, she was jealous of the thought of Mac and Sophie. That was crazy. She forced herself to put on her best nonchalant face.

"I don't know. One of you is about all I can handle right now." He chuckled a delightfully deep laugh, and the side of his mouth quirked up into a smile.

A smile she ignored.

He pulled the truck off the road directly behind her car and let the headlights illuminate the area. He climbed out of the truck, and she scampered out of her side. They walked through the swaths of light toward her car, and she popped the trunk while Mac did a careful perusal as he walked around her car.

"I think we have a problem." He walked back around to stand beside her at the trunk.

"Yes, I know. I have a flat. But I have a spare in the trunk."

"Well, it looks like you have two flats. Must have hit something when you pulled off the road or maybe you ran over something, but you've got two flats."

"And one spare tire."

"That about sums it up." Mac nodded and looked at her.

"I…"

"Looks like I'll be taking you into town again." He closed her trunk.

"But—"

"I don't see that either of us has any choice."

"I hate to put you out again."

"It's no problem."

She couldn't tell if there was any sincerity in his answer or not. But he was right, she had no choice.

They walked back to his truck and she started to slip in the mud. In that crazy moment of oh-my-gosh-I'm-going-to-fall, he deftly caught her and kept his hand on her elbow as they crossed the distance. She ungracefully clambered into his truck, her muddy shoes slipping as she entered the vehicle. Great, now she was covering the inside of his truck in mud, too. He was going to regret ever stopping to help her this afternoon.

He put the truck into gear and they headed back toward Sweet River Falls.

And she needed to ask him another favor, too. This night was going swimmingly. "Could we stop by the school for a minute on the way to my house? I hate to ask you, but I really need to pick up some papers to grade tonight. I forgot to grab them when I was there for the meeting. Do you think we could stop at the school on the way to my house?"

The low light from the dash faintly illuminated his face. He paused long enough for her to get a good look at his reluctant expression. "No problem. This seems to be my day to escort you around town."

"If it's a bother…"

"I said it wasn't a problem."

"Your words said no problem, but your face said it was a problem."

"What are you? A shrink now too, as well as a prim and proper school teacher, soon to be mayor?"

"Don't get so testy. I'm sorry I asked."

"I said okay." He practically growled the words at her.

She felt like spitting nails at him. She was going to ignore him for the rest of the ride. She deliberately turned to watch out the window on her side of the truck. She was just going to pretend he wasn't there. Really.

After about five minutes, she was mad. He was ignoring her. The nerve of the man. The sooner she got home the better. Then with any luck, they'd never cross paths again. They'd gone years without seeing each other. Surely they could go years more.

They pulled up to the school, and she jerked her door open before he even had a chance to try to open it for her. "I'll be right back."

"I'll walk you inside. It looks pretty dark in there."

"I'm sure the janitor is still in there cleaning. I see some lights on."

"I'd feel better if you'd let me walk you inside."

"I'm perfectly capable..." She let out a sigh of acceptance. She didn't know why everything he said to her got under her skin. "Fine. Thank you." She turned on her heels and headed for the door with determined strides.

How in the world did he get himself into this building twice in one day? After all these years. And why did she have a bee in her bonnet? She seemed to be madder than a wet hen as his friend JT used to say. Did she really think he'd let her walk into a dark building alone?

The thought did occur to him maybe she

thought it was more dangerous to go inside with him than alone. His not-so-sterling reputation did that kind of thing to people. He looked closely at her to see if she looked nervous. No, she looked irritated. Good. He found he liked getting under her skin.

He reached for the door. "Here let me get that for you."

She entered the school and nodded down the hall to the left. "My classroom is right down there."

"I'll join you in a second. Need to use the bathroom."

"The teacher's bathrooms are right down the other hallway."

"I remember."

She nodded and headed toward her classroom.

Okay, so he'd admit to himself, he'd always wanted to go into the teacher's bathroom. They got their own separate one. He pushed open the door to the men's room and laughed. It was exactly like the boys' bathroom. Exactly. All that wondering for nothing.

When he'd been at school there had only been two male teachers anyway. Three stalls. Seemed like overkill.

He walked out and flicked out the light. He crossed in front of the office. How many times had he sat there, scuffing his shoes on the floor, waiting for the principal, Mr. Thompson, to send for him for yet another punishment for some infraction of the rules? He stood there looking through the window into the room.

The chair he'd waited on was right by the window between the hall and the office. Same black faux-leather chair. A little more worn from squirming behinds waiting to see the principal. The hair on the back of his neck prickled with remembrance. He could still feel the stares of the other kids as they passed by the window. He could still hear their joking remarks about him.

Shaking away the memories, he walked down the hall in the direction Beth had headed. He looked down at the floor. How did schools find such ugly tile for the floors? Dirty specks of brown and gray. Didn't it ever wear out? It was the same ugly tile that had been there when he'd gone to school here. Maybe schools had some kind of code they followed that insisted on hideous tile.

A light shone from one of the classrooms. The bright, cheerful feel to the room surprised him as he walked in. Travel posters covered one whole wall. A row of plants sat on the windowsill. Instead of the regular industrial clock with a black rim, a bright clock with a cat face and ears sat on top of the blackboard.

A full bookshelf stood in the corner. He wandered back toward it while Beth collected her papers. A small sign on the bookshelf said *feel free to borrow, but please return.*

He glanced up as he heard Beth approaching.

"Those are my books. I figure it's better they're here being read than sitting at my house. So far the kids have been very good at bringing them back."

"Doesn't the school supply their books?"

"Well, these are extra ones. I try to pick up books at the bookstore when I see one of my kids is especially interested in some subject. I haunt yard sales too, looking for books the kids might enjoy."

He watched as her eyes lit up as she spoke about her students. "You really like teaching, don't you?"

"I've always wanted to be a teacher. I can't imagine doing anything else."

"Won't being a mayor interfere with your teaching?"

He watched as she stood there for a moment then frowned. "I'd be able to help the town, the same way I help my students. Larry Smith was a practicing lawyer when he was mayor. The position is only part-time. I think I can do a good job at both. I do love teaching the kids, and I think I'd make a good mayor."

Her eyes held a wistful look. He wasn't convinced she *should* get what she wanted. She seemed like such a caring, motivated teacher. The world needed more of them. How was she going to add all the responsibilities of being a mayor in with being a teacher?

"Are you sure about this mayor job?"

"Of course I'm sure. Otherwise, I wouldn't be running for it."

"Sometimes the best things that happen to us are unanswered prayers." Mac slipped a book he'd been looking at back on the shelf.

She set her shoulders straight and pinned him with what he was sure was her best teacher glare. "I really don't think you're quite ready to judge what is best for me, after your grand knowledge of knowing me for one day."

He wanted to tell her he knew her better than she thought but just nodded his head. Ruffling her feathers was one thing, but an all-out argument was quite a different matter. Sometimes people just had to get what they wished for to find out it wasn't really what they wanted after all.

She stalked to the door, then turned to face him. "Are you ready to go?" Her voice held exaggerated patience.

"Mm-hmm."

She flicked off the lights, and he followed her out the door.

He trailed behind her as she adjusted her stack of papers and fished around in her purse, probably looking for the car keys she had so much trouble keeping track of.

"Just a second. I think I left my keys on my desk. Wait here. I'll be right back." Beth turned back toward her classroom.

Mac lounged against the lockers, feeling the cold steel press against his back. Familiar feeling, yet different.

All of a sudden, bright lights flooded around him and he was surrounded by police. "Hold it right there," a voice commanded from just past the lights.

"What seems to be the matter?"

"Don't move, buddy."

Mac felt the familiar apprehension creep up

his spine. This gosh awful school. He was always getting in trouble at this blasted school.

"Look, officer. I'm not doing anything."

"Save it." One of the policemen approached him with his hand resting on his gun at his side. "Why don't you tell us why you're in here."

"Now don't get trigger happy. I'm just waiting for Miss Cassidy. She's in her classroom."

Mac heard Beth's welcome voice from behind the crowd of police. "Is there a problem here?"

One of the officers turned toward her. "This man says he's with you."

"He is." She walked through what felt to him like an immense crowd and came to stand beside him.

He took one look at her face and almost smiled. She looked like a mother hen protecting her chick.

"We got a call from the janitor that he saw a strange man poking around in the school."

"Mr. McKenna was just escorting me in the building to pick up some of my papers."

"Well, we've been having some problems with petty theft and vandalism at the school. We thought maybe we were going to catch them in the act this time."

"Well, you've made a mistake. I believe you owe Mr. McKenna an apology."

"Look, lady, we're only doing our job."

"Show some respect for the woman, guys," Mac warned.

"Don't cause any more trouble, buddy," the officer shot back. "We could bring you down to headquarters for questioning in the thefts, you know."

Mac looked down, surprised to feel the heat of Beth's hand resting on his forearm.

"Let's not get all upset." She flashed a charming smile at the young officer in front of her.

He almost laughed out loud at the man's reaction. Mac was sharp enough to know that smile was plastered insincerely across her face. The pressure of her hand kept him from showing any reaction.

A man clad in coveralls approached them. "That you, Miss Cassidy?"

"Yes, Mr. Dudley. I'm sorry to worry you. I was just popping in to pick up some papers."

The janitor nodded. "I'm sorry to have

brought in the police, ma'am. I just thought someone was busting in. I didn't see it was you."

"That's okay." Beth turned toward the young officer again. He'd taken his hand off his gun and nervously adjusted his cap. "If this is all settled, I believe Mr. McKenna and I will leave."

"Sorry for the inconvenience, ma'am."

Beth nodded and turned to Mac. "Would you carry these for me please?" She dumped her stack of papers into his arms as if to prove he really was there to help her.

He followed her to the door. Behind him he heard the officers and the janitor talking in low voices. But not low enough.

"Wonder whatever Miss Cassidy is doing with that character. Sure doesn't seem her type."

CHAPTER 4

Not my type indeed! Beth bristled at the callous comment, hoping Mac didn't hear it. She might agree he wasn't her type, but there was no use hurting his feelings.

"I'm sorry about all that mess in there." She felt his hand brush past her to push open the door.

"It's not your fault."

"But if I hadn't asked you to stop here, it wouldn't have happened."

"But I insisted on going in with you."

She turned to face him and grinned. "Okay, it's all your fault then."

He grinned back. "You sure are a handful of trouble."

Beth grinned. "That's what my mom used to

say about boys like you." She could just hear her mother's voice in the back of her mind. *Trouble with a capital T.*

"She might have been right, you know."

"I don't think so. You're not at all like I imagined."

"You spent time imagining what I was like?"

"I mean… I just figured… oh, never mind." There he stood with that lopsided grin spread across his face. She wasn't sure if she wanted to smack the grin off his face or trail her fingers along his smirking lips. She remembered those lips. How could she forget them?

It had been so long ago, but she still remembered every detail. She had been fourteen or fifteen. Never kissed a boy in her life. She had taken a shortcut home, through the woods behind the school. She'd seen him sitting under a tree with his head in his hands. The sun had highlighted the blackness of his hair, head bowed against some unknown demon. She'd walked quietly up to him and he'd looked up in surprise.

She still remembered their exact words. "You okay?" she asked him.

"Sure, why wouldn't I be?"

"I just thought…"

"Does your mama know you cut through these woods all alone?"

She took a quick step back and put on a brave front. "No, not that it matters."

He shook his head. "Girls. Not a lick of sense in their heads."

"I beg your pardon?"

"I'll walk you to the edge of the woods."

"I can find my own way."

"I'm sure you can. I'll walk you anyway."

She turned then and stalked away from him. Away from his piercing look. Away from his steel blue eyes. Away from trouble. With a capital T.

She felt him following her and picked up her pace, hurrying but trying not to seem like it. Then on the last hill before reaching the edge of the woods, she'd slipped. She slid down the path, spilling books and papers in her wake.

He quietly picked up each paper and book as he climbed down the hill after her. "Here." He gook a clean bandanna out of his pocket. He reached out and slid her skirt up. Just a little. He must have seen the fear in her eyes. "I just wanted to clean up the blood. I won't hurt you."

She nodded silently. With the gentlest touch,

he wiped the blood from her knees, then settled her skirt back into place.

He held out his hand to help her up. She didn't know how long she sat there, spilled flat on her rear, hair tangled with twigs. She finally reached out to take his hand, and he pulled her to her feet.

"Ow." She stumbled against him, clutching his jacket to keep her balance.

"You okay?"

"My ankle." She muttered a forbidden swear word.

"Girls shouldn't swear."

"Oh, and you're an expert on girls I suppose."

"I suppose."

She remembered willing herself to ignore the pain and trying to take a step. She cried out in pain and blinked back the tears.

"I'll help you."

She nodded then, too tired to argue. She just wanted to be home. He wrapped his arm around her and practically carried her up the hill. She still remembered how strong his arm felt. How safe she felt. At the same time, a flutter of apprehension coursed through her for enjoying the feel of his arms wrapped securely around her.

But she instinctively knew he'd get her home okay. As long as her mother didn't see them coming… Then she'd be dead.

He deposited her on her front step of their cabin at the lodge and piled her school books beside her. As he started to walk away, she'd grabbed his hand. The electric charge that raced through her caught her off guard. He'd swung around, stared into her eyes, and bent over and kissed her. She still remembered how it felt. His lips hard against hers, but gentle. And she remembered kissing him back.

He'd pulled away then, nodded, and hurried away. His nod somehow felt like some kind of dismissal.

She still remembered the feel of his lips, now, while she stared at them in the dim light of the parking lot. She had kissed lots of boys… men…. since then. But she still remembered her first kiss.

He probably had no idea.

He probably didn't even remember it.

He probably didn't know it had been her.

SHE PROBABLY DIDN'T REMEMBER that day. Years ago. The day he'd kissed those inviting pink lips. Tender, inexperienced, and seeking lips. Those lips had kissed him back, he remembered that. With a promise of something more. Questioning. Probing. Pulling him closer.

He had broken off the kiss, turned, and sped away. Racing away in slow motion. From the magnetic pull that had threatened to yank him back.

Mac shook the old memory clear and walked her back to the truck. Without a word, he silently climbed inside and started the engine.

He needed to get her home.

Out of his truck.

She gave him her address, and after what seemed like way too long, he pulled into her driveway.

"Thanks for your help." She looked over and smiled at him.

"It wasn't a problem," Mac lied. It certainly *had* been a problem. All these thoughts and feelings of inadequacy that he'd so carefully hidden away for so many years were now back in full force. Swarming around him. Reminding him. Calling him names. He was never going to get away from it.

"Well, thank you. I mean it." She reached for her papers and slid out of the truck.

He felt like he should offer to walk her to her door, but he didn't. He did sit in the drive and make sure she got safely inside. She turned and gave him a quick wave before she slipped inside the door.

He shook his head to clear his thoughts, feeling amazingly like he remembered feeling when he sped away after kissing her all those long years ago.

He shoved his hand through his hair in exasperation. Fool. A woman like that wanted nothing to do with him. They lived in different worlds. And he had made a pretty good world for himself. He sure didn't need any prissy school teacher, even a cute one with a sassy smile, coming into his life and messing up his organized, predictable world.

Certainly not one who wanted to be mayor of a town that had given him nothing but trouble. He was done with Sweet River Falls. Completely.

He threw the truck into reverse, pulled out of her drive, and he headed back to his own safe world.

CHAPTER 5

Nora and Annie sat out by Lone Elk Lake, watching the sun set over the water. Two best friends enjoying the tranquility and a few minutes out of their busy schedules. "It's so wonderful here." Annie sighed. "You're very lucky to be able to walk right out your door and see this view. I do love living in my father's house, but this view is magical."

"It is. I do worry about all the talk about development of the land. I hope it doesn't really happen." Nora frowned.

"I'll do anything to help you to stop it. Surely the townspeople don't want that happen. That's why zoning laws were put into place."

Nora smiled at Annie. Sometimes it helped

just to sit and talk things over with her. She'd known her almost her whole life. Friends like that were something to treasure. "I hope you're right." Nora watched a glittery ray of light dance across the ripples of the lake. "I do worry about Beth though."

"What do you mean?" Annie turned, her brow furrowed.

"I... I think she's running for mayor because she's hoping to stop Dobbs. Stop anyone from rezoning the lake. She's trying to help me. Help preserve the beauty of the lake and the peacefulness of it. Save the lake, to save the atmosphere and specialness of the lodge."

"I'm sure she does want to help you and save all this." Annie flung her arm wide.

"I won't have the same clientele or people staying at the lodge if the lake gets condos and motor boats. My customers come for the peace and quiet. We get so many people who come back year after year. If the lake changes... well, everything will change."

"Well, maybe Beth can help prevent it if she gets elected for mayor."

Nora looked at her friend and took a deep breath. "The thing is... I don't think that Beth really *wants* to be mayor. I think she's just running to help save the lake and save the lodge."

"Do you really think that?" Annie frowned.

"I really do. But when Beth gets her mind set on something, there is no talking her out of it." Nora leaned back in her chair, and they sat side by side until the last of the sun slipped behind the mountains and the first stars came out, highlighting the perfect peace of Lone Elk Lake.

LATER THAT EVENING, Annie stood in the doorway of the master bedroom of her father's house.

No, it was her house.

She always had to remind herself. Her father was gone, and the house was hers. Well, hers and Nick's now.

She turned as she heard Nick approaching. He wore a welcoming smile, one she'd quickly come to look forward to when he came home each day.

He gave her a quick hug. "Hi, sweetheart. What are you doing standing here in the hallway?"

"I think it's time we did something with this bedroom." Annie pointed to her father's room. She hadn't changed anything since he'd died. She even had some of his clothes in the closet. Same quilt on the bed. If she pulled open the bedside table drawer, she'd find his old worn Bible and a stack of three-by-five cards and a pen that he always had near to jot notes on.

The heat of a lone tear trickled down her cheek, but she knew in her heart it was time to move on.

"We don't have to do this." Nick reached for her hand.

"It's silly that we're squeezed into my tiny room when there's this perfectly roomy master suite."

"I'm fine where we are."

"No, it's time. I know it is." She looked at Nick. "But… well, can we paint it and make it look… different?"

"Anything you want."

Annie looked at him, her heart swelling with love. It might have taken them years to get to this point, but she loved this man so much. She stepped into the master suite, and he came to stand beside her. She looked around the room. "I think some light sage paint on the walls would brighten it up. New curtains. I promise not to make them too girly." She grinned at Nick.

"I'd appreciate that." He winked at her.

"We'll get a nice down comforter for the bed. I'll clear out the closet and chest of drawers."

"You're sure?" He touched her chin and tilted her face up.

She looked into his eyes. "I'm sure."

"As you wish. But you know I'd live in a barn with you, if that's what you wanted." He tossed a teasing grin at her.

"I think we can do a bit better than an old cold barn and a hayloft."

"A nice comfortable bed is always good," he said agreeably and took her in his arms.

She wrapped her arms around his waist and leaned against him, listening to his heart beat as she pressed her cheek against his chest. She pulled back and looked into his eyes.

"I love you so much."

"I love you too, Mrs. Chambers. I've never been happier."

CHAPTER 6

Beth finished her morning run, dodging the puddles from the previous night's storm. She grabbed the once-a-week town newspaper as she sped up the walkway to her house. She pulled the cord with her house key from around her neck and started to unlock the door. She'd learned that hanging the key around her neck was the only way to make sure she still had it when she got back from her run. She momentarily felt like a latch-key kid.

The door swung wide as soon as she grabbed the doorknob.

Darn-it-all, she'd forgotten to lock the door again. She could have sworn she remembered locking it as she left. Beth could almost hear her mother's admonition. *You might live in a small town, but a woman living alone with her children should always lock her door.*

She was getting better at remembering to lock it. She was.

Usually.

Beth pushed open her door and stepped inside. One quick look assured her she'd been wrong.

Totally wrong.

She hadn't left the door open. Someone had broken in.

One quick glance took in the broken vase, the knocked over furniture, the drawer from the desk by the front door dripping its contents onto the rug.

She backed out quickly. Out to safety. This was not something she was going to deal with alone.

Beth turned and ran down the street and around the corner to Main Street and raced up the back stairs of the Brooks Gallery to Sophie's apartment above it. She burst into her friend's apartment. "Sophie," she shouted as she sprinted through the door. The thought flitted through her mind that Sophie really should remember to lock her door, too.

Sophie came rushing out of the bathroom tying her bathrobe around her.

"What is it?" She wrapped a towel around her dripping hair.

"Someone—" Beth gasped for air and bent over to catch her breath. "Broke—into my house."

Sophie grabbed the landline phone off the wall and pressed it into Beth's hands. "Call the police."

Beth nodded. Most people kept a landline here in Sweet River Falls because cell service could be so spotty in the mountains. She gasped in more air while she punched in the phone number for the police, listed conveniently on the memo board by the phone. Why do people list the police number by the phone? It's not like they have to call them all the time. Her thoughts bounced around. She forced her attention back to the matter at hand. The one she was trying to forget.

Daniel Smith answered the phone at the police station. Good. He'd had a crush on her in grade school. He'd want to help her. Her thoughts were ricocheting all over.

"This is Beth Cassidy." She was still fighting for breath. "My house has been broken into."

Beth turned and looked at Sophie. "No, I'm at Sophie's. Okay, I'll wait here for you. No, I promise I'm not going in there alone. No, not with Sophie either. Okay. Bye."

Sophie came over, pushed her down in the kitchen chair, and pressed a hot cup of coffee into her hands. "Calm down. Now tell me what happened."

"I came back from my run. The door swung open. I thought I'd left it open again. I could hear my mom lecturing me." Beth rubbed her shoulder. "But I looked in and the place is trashed."

"Geez, Beth. That's creepy. Who would want to trash the place?" Sophie toweled her hair and sunk into the chair next to Beth.

"I don't know. Money, I guess. I didn't go in long enough to see if anything was missing."

"Good choice. Let the police check it out first."

Beth still struggled to get herself under control. Like she needed this right now. "Oh, I better call my mom and stop her before she brings the boys home. I don't want them walking into a house full of police."

"Okay, call her and let me run and get

dressed and I'll come over to the house with you when the police say it's okay."

Beth punched in her mother's number and drummed her fingers on the counter as she counted the rings. No answer. She tried her mother's cell phone. Still no answer, but with such come and go service in the mountains she wasn't surprised. "Sophie, get a move on. I can't reach Mom. I want to get there before she does."

IT WAS TOO LATE.

Beth could see her mom's car in front of the house as they approached. Her mother was arguing with poor Daniel Smith.

"Beth!" Her mother came rushing up to her. "What is this town coming to? Nothing but hoodlums. Are you okay?"

"I'm fine." Her boys came running up to her. She encircled them in a big hug, grateful they'd been away from home when the house was broken into.

"Mom. You okay?" Worry creased Connor's face.

"I'm fine, really." She quickly reassured him.

"They won't let us look inside. Can we go inside? Can we?" Trevor started to pull her toward the house.

"Not until the police are finished looking around."

"Didn't I tell you to lock your door?" Her mother gave her the world famous what-did-I-tell-you look. Suddenly she felt like she was ten years old.

"Mom, I was sure I locked the door this morning."

"Well, young Daniel here says there is no sign of forced entry."

Beth was just sure she remembered locking the door when she left for her run. She'd made up a little saying to remember it. Katydid. K. D. Did it. Keys, door, did it. She was sure she had chanted that as she left.

"Beth, there is no sign of anyone forcing the lock. You sure you locked it?" Daniel came up to her, looking official in his uniform with a notebook in his hand. Quite different than the gawky kid with ill-fitting pants and black glasses in high school.

"I really think I did."

"Well, who all has a key?"

"Mom, of course." Beth smiled weakly at

her mother, who did not seem amused. "Sophie. And both the boys."

She turned toward her sons. "Are your backpacks in Gram's car?"

They nodded.

"Go get them and let's be sure the keys are still in them."

The boys solemnly trailed to the car and retrieved their backpacks. Each of them looked worried that they might have lost the keys in spite of the fact that she regularly admonished them about the importance of not misplacing them. She certainly didn't want them to inherit her ability to lose things...

"We both have them." Connor sounded relieved.

"Any other key?" Daniel questioned again.

Beth was loath to even mention it, but she had to admit that Mac McKenna had had her keys for hours last night. But he'd have no reason to trash her house. He wasn't the type. And what? He'd taken her key and rushed to make a copy of it?

"Beth?" Sophie looked at her carefully. "Didn't Mac McKenna have your keys last night?"

Well, there was no way to keep him out of it

now. "For a bit. But he'd have no reason to do this. I must have left the door unlocked."

Only she was *pretty* certain she hadn't.

"Well, I think we'll just pay a visit to Mr. McKenna and see what he was up to this morning anyway." Daniel almost swaggered with authority.

"Daniel, leave him be. He didn't do this."

But what did she really know about Mac anyway? She didn't really know him. He seemed kind. Not at all the sort of person to do this.

Or would he?

She didn't need this complication right now.

MAC SLICED his knife through another corrugated box. He stepped on the box to smash it and tossed it onto the growing pile of flattened boxes. He'd have to make a trip to the recycling center soon.

He heard footsteps coming around the corner of the building and paused with the knife still suspended in the air.

"Drop the knife."

Mac turned to see two officers standing there with their hands suspended in the air at their sides. He was not oblivious of their guns resting in their holsters inches from their hands.

This was getting to be a habit…

"What do you want?" Mac stood there, still holding the knife poised above the next box.

"I said to drop the knife." The younger officer fidgeted with the butt of his gun.

"Is there a problem?" Mac slowly closed the knife but continued to hold it in his hand.

"Set it down." An officer who looked vaguely familiar nodded his head toward the knife in his hand.

Mac set the knife down on the ground. "Is there a problem?" He slowly repeated his question in a tone usually reserved for grilling a wayward child.

"We have some questions for you."

"Ask them, then. I need to get back to work."

"Where were you this morning?"

"Right here."

"Anyone see you?"

"Doubt it. We don't open until eleven."

The young officer still fidgeted with his hand near his gun.

"You mind telling your young partner there to get his hand off his gun?" Mac nodded toward the nervous officer. He looked barely old enough to be out of high school, much less old enough to be carting around a gun with authoritative immunity.

"Joey." The familiar looking cop gestured to his partner, who slowly took his hand away from his gun.

"I understand you had Miss Cassidy's keys yesterday."

"Yep."

"Well, in a strange coincidence, her house was broken into this morning. No sign of forced entry. Right after you've had her keys."

"Her house was broken into this morning? Is she okay?" Mac heard the concern in his voice and that fact alone surprised him.

"She wasn't home at the time."

Smith, that was it. The familiar looking cop was somebody Smith who had gone to school at the same time he did. "Look, Officer Smith." Mac paused as he saw surprise in the man's eyes. "I've been here all morning. So you're looking in the wrong direction."

"Seems like quite the coincidence though, don't you think?"

"You can think what you want. I've been here all morning. I suggest you two just move along. I've answered your questions. I've got work to do." Mac could feel his muscles tense. Beth Cassidy had been nothing but trouble since she'd popped back into his life yesterday. *Two* encounters with the police. It was like being back in school. Always the suspect. Accused of anything and everything that went wrong.

"We have a few more questions."

"And I'm finished answering them. Unless you have some kind of warrant?" Mac wasn't sure why he was being so stubborn, except that he was tired of being presumed guilty. He thought he'd left that lifestyle a long time ago. He had a new life here a couple of towns over from where he'd grown up. He was accepted here. He fit in. The people of Mountain Grove came to his tavern, trusted him, even liked him. He had no desire to get dragged back into his never-fit-in lifestyle in Sweet River Falls.

"Come on, Joey." The Smith guy gave Mac one more good, long stare. "We might be back with more questions."

Mac didn't even bother to answer him as he deliberately reached down to pick up the knife. He watched the men retreat around the corner of the building. After a minute, he heard their car start and pull out onto the roadway.

Now he had some unfinished business with Beth. There was no way she was going to drag him down or pull him back into the life of an outsider. Label him as a troublemaker. He was finished with that life and finished with any entanglement with Beth Cassidy.

Except to go confront her about accusing him of breaking into her house.

CHAPTER 7

Beth swept up the dirt from the ficus tree planter the intruder had knocked over. It was a ridiculously heavy planter. It couldn't have been knocked over accidentally.

She dropped a dustpan of dirt into the trashcan she'd brought into the house. Everything was such a mess. She'd ended up taking a day off from work. She'd called the principal of the school and explained the situation. She hated to take a personal day—the last thing she needed was to look irresponsible about her duties—but she wanted to get things straightened up before the boys came home from school. Unfortunately, that wasn't going to happen. It was just too big of a job. Thankfully, the boys' room hadn't been disturbed.

Her bedroom had, though. The drawers all pulled out. Closet gaping open with clothes tossed on the floor. She had methodically been going through and washing every item of clothing the intruder had tossed. She couldn't stand the thought of putting on clothes some stranger had touched while invading her home.

Beth repeatedly shook away the sense of unease that kept creeping up on her while she worked on the house. She'd made the boys promise to go over to Gram's house after school. Sophie had said that she'd be over as soon as she could to help.

Beth heard heavy booted steps on the front porch. Probably the officers returning with yet more questions. She paused in response to the knock at the door, then shook her head. The intruder wouldn't come back and *knock*. She tugged open the door.

Mac McKenna stood planted firmly in the doorway. His face was lined with a hard edge. His eyes burned coldly. She shivered.

"Mr. McKenna."

He looked past her into the chaos of her house. "You think I did this?" Mac's voice was low. "The officers you sent to grill me seemed pretty certain I'm responsible for breaking into your home."

"I'm sorry about dragging you into this mess. They asked who had keys. There was no sign of a break-in."

"So, of course, you thought of me immediately."

"No, I told them to leave you alone. I don't think you were responsible." *Did she?*

"But you had to tell them I had your keys for a while? You thought I ran out and made a duplicate of them or something?"

"Well, what was I supposed to do? I have two boys to worry about too. You did have the keys. I won't have my instincts of trusting you overwhelm my responsibility to them."

A brief look crossed his face as though he almost understood her position. The boys would always come first with her. But she really didn't think he was involved in this. Which brought her to another problem.

Who *was* involved?

Mac wasn't involved in this. He wasn't. She could just feel it. Besides, Daniel Smith had dropped by after questioning Mac and told her that Mac said he'd been at his bar the whole morning. No witnesses, though...

"Here, I remembered I had this. Came to town to show you." He pulled out a crumpled paper from his pocket. "A delivery I got this morning. See?"

She slowly reached out and took the paper. It was time stamped seven a.m. He'd signed for the delivery, too.

She'd known he wasn't involved. She shook away the last of her doubts. Her instincts rarely failed her, and she instinctively felt Mac had grown into a kind man and not someone who would break into her home.

She handed the paper back to him. She'd almost swear that the briefest look of hurt crossed his face before he turned to leave.

"No, wait." She took a step and reached out to touch his arm. "Come in."

He turned back toward the door. "Are you sure?"

"Mr. McKenna, don't be silly. Come in."

MAC CROSSED through the doorway and entered a new world. Even with the scattered mess, the room conveyed a feeling of welcome. This was a home, not just a house.

He carefully wiped his boots on the mat as he entered. His slow perusal of the front room took in the brightly covered couch. It looked worn and comfortable. A print of two Adirondack chairs on the edge of a lake hung over the fireplace. Sun streamed in the windows.

Juxtaposed against the feeling of homeyness was the background feeling of invasion. "Let me help." The words just sprang from him, uninvited.

"No, I couldn't ask that of you."

"I'd like to." He could tell she was tired. The strain of the day showed clearly on her face.

She nodded slowly. "Thanks."

He worked quietly by her side for over an hour. Asking a question or two regarding what she wanted done with this or that. Picking up broken pieces of dishes and glass from broken pictures.

"It looks more like someone just wanted to trash the place than a burglary." Mac looked around and frowned.

"That's what the police said too."

"Any ideas on who would want to do this? A disgruntled student?"

"I teach third grade. I just don't see this as the work of a third grader."

"No, probably not."

Mac glanced around the front room. Everything looked back in place to him. Books back on the shelves. Desk back in order. Pillows placed carefully on the couch. He watched as Beth shoved her hair back from her face. Exhaustion creased the corners of her eyes.

"Mind if we take a little break?" he asked.

Relief showed on her face. "Not at all. I'll get us some tea."

Mac followed her into the kitchen. It was still a disaster. Maybe this hadn't been such a good idea after all. Beth just stood there in the center of the room looking around at the spilled drawers and open cabinets.

"Water is fine. I'll get it. You go back and sit in the front room."

Beth nodded gratefully. "The glasses are setting by the sink." She pointed to the counter. "But…"

"I'll wash them out first," he completed her thought. He could only imagine the feeling of invasion of having someone go through all of your things. He quickly washed the glasses, filled them with ice and water, and returned to the front room.

Beth had sat on an easy chair, her feet

propped up on a footrest. She looked up as he crossed to the chair beside her.

"Here." Mac handed her a glass and sank down into the overstuffed cushions on a chair next to her. "You doing okay?"

"I'm just tired."

"It's probably the emotional strain more than the physical work."

"Probably. I just can't figure out who would do this. Or why."

"Maybe it was just some random act."

"I don't know if that makes me feel better or worse." She glanced at her watch. "The boys will be here soon. I really should get to work on straightening up the kitchen before they get here."

"You need a break."

"What I need is for things to fall into place in my life instead of fight me at every turn."

Whoa. Now there was a statement with far-reaching implications. He wasn't sure he wanted to open that can of worms.

But he did anyway.

"Things a little tough for you right now?"

She sat and stared at the moisture running down the sides of her glass before she answered. "Well, there is the fact that my ex-husband left me for a barely out of high school girl. He rarely has time for the boys anymore. Or the minor detail that the house got broken into. Or the stress of worrying about what happens to my mother's lodge on Lone Elk Lake if Dobbs gets his way." She shifted in her chair. "But it's not so much the big things that are getting to me. It's the constant trail of little things. The flat tire. Okay, two of them. Worrying about balancing my job and still having enough time with the boys. Finding the money to pay all the bills. Constantly having to say no to the boys for things they ask for. I swear that sometimes just hauling the garbage out to the street or figuring out what's for dinner is enough to put me over the edge."

The sunlight danced through the window, highlighting her legs first with light, then shade. He had no idea what to say to this woman. She carried a lot of responsibility on her shoulders. The stress of the break-in would just add to her burdens. His thoughts jumped all around. He figured it was best not to tell her that marrying that loser quarterback from high school was not one of her smarter decisions.

"Maybe you need to get away for a few days. Take a break."

"That would just make me further behind."

"Maybe it would be worth it, just to step back and reevaluate your priorities."

"I just don't have the luxury to do that."

"Maybe adding the responsibilities of being the mayor might not be the smartest thing right now." He persisted even though he wasn't sure he was saying the right thing. Or that it was the right time to say it.

She set her glass down on the table with a clatter. "You have no idea what's best. What's best is someone besides James Weaver becomes mayor. Someone who will fight the development of looming high-rise condominiums on Lone Elk Lake. I grew up there. I can't bear to see the quiet beauty of the place ruined with yet another noisy condo complex, busy marina, and constant stream of people who don't appreciate these last few untouched lakes in the area. They don't appreciate the peace. The quiet. The pure…"

She slashed her hand across her cheek, and he was pretty sure he'd missed the fact a tear had escaped.

"I'm sorry, Beth. I didn't mean to upset you. I can see being mayor is important to you."

"It is."

"Then I guess it's something you should do." He leaned back in his chair as she picked up her water glass again.

He didn't miss that she still watched him warily over the rim of the glass as if worried he'd question again the wisdom of her adding yet more responsibilities to her life.

CHAPTER 8

Nora popped into Bookish Cafe with just enough time to grab a coffee with Annie before heading to pick up the boys from school for Beth. She'd offered to keep them overnight again to give Beth time to finish cleaning up her house, but Beth had insisted the boys come home and that she'd have everything finished before school let out.

"Nora, I heard about the break-in at Beth's. Is she okay?" Annie wrapped Nora in a hug.

"She's a bit shaken. The house is a mess, but she stayed home today to clean it all up and put things back in order. I offered to help, but she said she would do it. You know how independent she can be."

"But she must be so upset. What's this town

coming to?" Annie led her over to the coffee bar and grabbed two mugs of steaming hot coffee. "Come, sit for a few."

Nora glanced at her watch. "I do have some time, but I need to go pick up the boys from school for Beth. I don't want to be late."

They headed upstairs to the new loft area to sit on some comfortable chairs by the window. Sweet River bubbled along the river walk outside the back of Annie's bookstore. Nora sank into the chair and took a grateful sip of her coffee. "Ah, that's good. Never did get my coffee this morning with all the hubbub of the break-in."

"Did they steal anything?" Annie sat beside her.

"I talked to Beth a bit ago and she can't find anything missing. She said it's more like they just wanted to trash her place."

Annie frowned. "That's strange."

"I know. I can't think of anyone who would want to do that."

"You think it's tied into her running for mayor?" Annie's forehead wrinkled. "Though, I can't even imagine James Weaver or any of his cronies stooping to that level."

"Well, I know Dobbs is mad that Beth is

running against James, but no, I can't imagine this is something he'd do either. The police are looking into it. I hope they turn up something."

Annie leaned back in her chair. "I remember when all the police had to handle here in Sweet River Falls were things like a rogue moose wandering through town and making sure some clueless tourist didn't mess with it."

Nora nodded. "Now there are break-ins to cars in the grocery parking lot and the occasional robbery of one of the stores here. I heard there has been some vandalism at the school, too."

"It's not quite the same Sweet River Falls we grew up in, is it?"

"I guess all towns change some. Though this isn't a change that I'd wish on any town." Nora shook her head.

"I heard Beth showed up at the council meeting with Mac McKenna." Annie leaned forward and rolled her eyes. "Gloria Edmunds came by to tell me that. She seemed to think it was the most *shocking thing ever* and would probably prevent Beth from ever being elected mayor.

"Gloria needs to learn to mind her own business."

"Like that would ever happen." Annie shrugged. "Anyway, didn't Mac McKenna go to school with Beth? Seems I remember he was a bit of a troublemaker."

"I wonder why Beth was with him? I haven't heard a word about him in years. If I remember right, he *was* a bit of a troublemaker in school, but I always got the impression he was more of a lost soul. I'll have to ask Beth about him." Nora glanced down at a couple walking along the river walk, hand in hand. This path along Sweet River had been a great addition to the town even if Dobbs had fought both her and Annie on it. She turned to her friend. "Anyway, let's talk about something more cheerful. How are you and Nick doing?"

Annie blushed and Nora laughed. "I take it things are going well with you two newlyweds?"

"I… I'm ridiculously happy. I told you he took that research job in Denver? He does some of the job remotely but goes into Denver a couple times a week. Home every night, though. We've gotten into a routine, kind of. It's very different to be living with someone after all those years of living alone."

"I bet."

"And I decided it's time to… well, let go of my father's room. We're going to move into the master suite. It's time. Nick is going to paint it and the master bath, and I ordered some new curtains. He just seemed to know that I needed the room to look different if we were going to move into it. I packed up the rest of Dad's clothes and gave them away. I finally decided it was time. Keeping the room as an empty shrine to my dad wasn't healthy. Besides, we can really use the space now that Nick moved in. So, next weekend we're going to move into the master suite."

Nora reached over and squeezed Annie's hand. "Good for you. Change is hard though, isn't it?"

"It sure is. Well, not the being with Nick part, but all the changes that have come about from marrying him."

"I'm just glad to see you so happy."

"I am. Sometimes I wonder what I did to deserve all this happiness. I'm just so content right now."

"And you deserve every bit of it." Nora took one last sip of her coffee. "I've got to run and pick up the boys. I think I'm going to try and convince Beth to come stay at the lodge with the boys for a few days until all this gets sorted out and they figure out who did this to her house."

"That's a great idea."

"If I can convince Miss Independent to do it." Nora sighed. Her daughter was a stubborn one, but she only had herself to blame. Like mother, like daughter. Well, they'd see who won this round.

"I'll catch up with you soon." Annie rose and collected their coffee mugs. "I should get back to work."

Nora left Bookish Cafe and ran through arguments in her head of reasons she could give her daughter to come stay at the lodge for a few days. Not that she had any illusions that her daughter would listen.

BETH SAT on the front steps with a bag packed with the boys' clothes. Even with Mac's help, she hadn't been able to get everything put back in order in the house. Her mother pulled up in front and Beth stood, grabbing the bag, and headed out to her car.

"Hi, Mom."

"Everything okay?" Her mother nodded at the bag.

"I was hoping the boys could stay with you at the lodge for the weekend."

"Of course they can. You're coming, too, right?"

"I think I'll stay here and… um… finish things." She looked pointedly at the boys, unwilling to explain what a disaster the house still was.

"Why don't you take a break and come with us?" Her mom got out of the car and reached for the bag. "You look exhausted."

"I'm fine, Mom. I really should stay and finish up."

"I'm gonna stay with Mom and help her," Connor piped up.

"No, you boys are going with Grams."

"But, Mom, you need help."

Just then she heard the front door open and turned to see Mac on the front step with another full trash bag in his hand.

"Who's he?" Trevor leaned forward to get a better look.

"He's a… friend. He's just here helping me."

"Is that Mac McKenna?" Her mom turned

and gave Mac a good long look then a brief wave.

Mac smiled and waved back, then headed over to the garbage can beside the garage.

"Yes. He stopped by."

"I haven't heard anything about him in years, but Annie said that he dropped you off at the council meeting last night."

A weak smile crossed her face. Nothing was missed in this small town. "I had a flat. He stopped and helped me and drove me back to town."

"Did you get your flat fixed?"

"I actually had two flats. I called Gary's Garage, and they went out today and towed it back to town. Ordered in new tires for me. Should be ready in the morning."

"I'm starving. You think Miss Judy has any cookies baked?" Connor asked.

Her mom smiled. "I'm sure she does. I better get you two back to the lodge and feed you before you starve to death."

"I hope they're oatmeal cookies. That's my favorite," Trevor said.

Her mom climbed into the car and set the boys' bag on the front passenger seat. "I wish you'd come with us."

"I really want to finish up here."

"I could come back and pick you up later."

"I'll be fine."

"Well, lock the door."

"I will, Mom. I will." She closed the car door for her mom and waved to the boys as they pulled away.

She turned and headed back inside. The sooner she got the mess picked up, the sooner she'd feel like she had some control back in her life.

Mac turned when he heard Beth enter the kitchen. "Get the boys off with your Mom?"

"I did. She wanted me to come stay with her for a few days, too, but I said no."

"I don't think that would be such a bad idea. At least until the police can find out who did this."

"I'm not going to be chased out of my home."

He still thought it was a good idea for her to go stay with her mother, but he wasn't going to push the issue. "Okay, well, I've almost finished up in here. Looks like they broke quite a few of your plates though."

"I guess I'll be shopping for new plates, then." She slowly shook her head.

"And this one mug." He held up a mug that was now in three pieces.

"Oh…" Beth's eyes filled with tears as she reached out and took the pieces from him. She collapsed onto a chair and silent tears streamed down her face.

"Beth?"

"I…" She gingerly set the pieces onto the table. "I'm sorry." She swiped at the tears. "This was my father's mug. See, it says Number One Daddy? I've kept it, and I use it only occasionally when I… well, when I feel the need to use it. On really bad days, or sometimes on really great days."

Mac remembered that Beth's father died when she was a young girl. He wasn't sure what age exactly, but young. "I'm so sorry." He knelt beside her and looked at the pieces. "I could try and glue it back together. Not sure it would still be drinkable, but at least you'd have it. I'm pretty good with my hands. Why don't you let me take it and try to fix it?"

"I'd appreciate that." She drew in a deep

breath. "I'm not usually so... fragile. I'm not really a crier."

"I think after the day you've had, you deserve to be whatever you want. Tears are sometimes very healing."

She gave him a thanks-for-understanding look, and his heart thumped in his chest. He didn't know why he was so eager to please her and make things easier on her. She certainly hadn't made things easier on him. She'd just complicated things. Visits from the police, memories of his terrible days at school, and... well, she'd kind of scrambled his thoughts, too.

And he didn't like it one bit.

Not one little bit.

And yet the tiny smile she gave him made it almost seem worthwhile.

CHAPTER 9

Beth looked at the man kneeling beside her, grateful for his help in cleaning the place, grateful for his offer to fix her father's mug. And if she were being honest with herself, grateful to have someone here with her while she dealt with everything.

This Mac McKenna was not the same one she went to school with. Of course, who was the same person after life threw its curves year after year?

"Beth?"

She heard the front screen door slam and Sophie call out.

"Back here."

Mac got to his feet as Sophie entered the kitchen. She stopped short. "Well, hi."

"Hi, Sophie." Mac smiled at her friend.

"Mac came by to… well, he stayed and helped me clean up."

Sophie looked around the kitchen. "Looks like he did a bang-up job." She turned to him and grinned. "Do you offer up cleaning help to everyone?"

"Usually just for people who have their home broken into," Mac said gravely with a twinkle in his eyes.

"Oh, well. I don't think I want someone to break into my apartment just to get your help then."

"Probably not." He cracked a lazy smile.

"Well, I came by to do the whole best friend helper thing, but it looks like I'm not needed." She turned to Beth. "You doing okay?"

"I'm fine. Really."

"You look horrible."

"Why, thanks, Sophie."

"I mean, exhausted. Upset. Worn out."

"You just keep cheering me up, don't you?"

"I'm doing my best." Sophie sank into a chair beside her and picked up a piece of the mug. "Oh, wow. Your dad's mug? I'm so sorry."

"Mac said he's going to try and fix it."

Sophie turned to Mac. "You're a man of

many hidden talents. Rescuer of damsels in distress when they have a flat, cleaner-upper, and fixer of mugs. I think I like you, Mac McKenna."

Mac grinned. "I think I like you too, Sophie. You think you could convince your friend to go stay with her mother for a few days?"

"I'm sitting right here, guys." Beth interrupted their discussion of her.

"See, he's smart, too." Sophie turned to Beth. "You should listen to him. That's good advice. Go stay with Nora."

"I'm staying here."

Sophie shrugged and turned to Mac. "That's her don't-argue-with-me voice. There's no use." She got to her feet. "Well, it looks like you and Mac have this under control. I have a hot date with a really good book and a glass of wine. It's been a long week."

"Thanks for stopping by." Beth started to get up.

"Nope, stay there. I'll let myself out. Call if you need anything. And I still think you should go to Nora's."

"Bye, Soph." She pointedly ended the conversation of where she should stay.

Her friend walked out of the room and the

front screen door slammed again behind her as she left.

Mac stood beside the table in the awkward silence blanketing the kitchen after Sophie's departure. Beth looked up at him. "I should feed you."

"What? No, that's okay."

"No, you've been here all day helping. Let me see what I can make us for dinner."

"You're exhausted."

"I am… but I'm starving, too." She slowly rose, but her feet screamed in protest.

"We could go out and grab a bite."

"No."

He raised an eyebrow at her quick refusal.

"I don't really want to see people or answer questions or field one more person asking if I'm okay." She walked over to the fridge and tugged it open. The cool rush of air washed around her in a weak attempt to revive her. At least whoever had trashed her place hadn't touched anything in the fridge. "I have burgers. Want to grill out?"

"That sounds fine. Where's the grill? I'll get it started."

"It's out back. A gas grill. I gave up on my charcoal grill after so many years of wildfires near here."

Mac left to start the grill, and she made the hamburger up into patties. She also had a head of lettuce for a salad, but that was about it. She carried the plate of burgers outside along with a long-handled spatula and two beers all balanced carefully on a tray.

"Ah, thanks." Mac reached for the tray and set it on a small table beside the grill looking quite at home with the barbecuing routine.

"Thought you might like a beer." She handed him one from the tray.

"And you were right. I'd love one." He took a long swig from the bottle.

"Are you sure you don't have to get back to your tavern?"

"Nah, it will be fine. I already called George and told him I'd be back later this evening." He pointed to a chair with the spatula. "Why don't you sit, put your feet up, and let me grill. You look like you're about to drop."

"Gee, thanks. You and Sophie are just full of compliments today."

"No, I MEAN—" He was hopeless with this woman. Always saying the wrong thing.

She smiled at him. A smile that lit up her eyes and made him want to do anything to keep that smile on her face. "I knew what you meant. I *am* tired. It was an emotionally draining day."

And just like that, she let him off the hook from his clumsy remark.

He watched her from the corner of his eye while he busied himself with the task of grilling the burgers. She sank onto a red metal chair and stretched out her long, jean-clad legs. She kicked off the leather loafers she had on and took a sip of her beer. Right from the bottle. For some reason, he liked that she drank from the bottle like he did instead of insisting on pouring the beer into a glass, which always seemed to him like such a waste. Though he did provide chilled glasses to anyone who requested one at his tavern, of course.

He glanced over at a tree house built in a large tree in the backyard. Beth's sons were evident everywhere he looked in her house, from baseball bats to two sets of sneakers by the door, to a video game controller sitting by the TV.

He didn't want to mention that his feelings were the tiniest bit hurt when she hadn't motioned him over to meet her boys or her mother, but then, that was silly. Why should she introduce him? He was just this random guy who had driven her home last night. Well, and came over to help her clean up. He frowned. Maybe she still didn't believe he wasn't involved in the break-in. Nope, that made no sense. She wouldn't have had him stay if she thought he was involved. He flipped the burgers.

"So, how old are your boys?" That was safe, right? Every parent liked to talk about their kids.

"Ten and eight. Connor is ten, Trevor eight. They're great kids even if they are a handful."

He knew she'd married the high school quarterback, what's-his-name. But there was no evidence of him being around and the only photo he'd seen of him was in the boys' bedroom when he'd brought a load of their toys back there for Beth. He couldn't quite remember the guy's name, but he'd been quite the arrogant jock, full of himself and his self-importance. He had no idea what Beth had seen in him though maybe she'd wised up and that was why he was no longer around.

He paused for a moment, wondering if he could ask. He drew in a breath and plunged in. "And their Dad? Is he around?"

"Scott? Sometimes. Not often."

Scott. Right, that was his name. Scott

Parker. But he'd noticed that Beth didn't go by the name Parker. She went by her maiden name, Cassidy. He figured it wasn't a good question to ask why, so he kept his question to himself.

"He's remarried now. Lives over near Vail and does some kind of PR for a resort there." She took a slow sip of her beer and looked out into the distance, seemingly lost in thought.

He didn't quite know what to say to all of that, so he busied himself with flipping the burgers again. "I think they're about ready."

She nodded and rose gracefully from her chair. "If you bring those in, I'll set the table and we can eat."

He took the burgers up, turned off the grill, and tidied the area.

He slipped through the screen door and set the platter on the table. Beth had set out two mismatched plates and bright red napkins. A nice salad and a couple of choices of salad dressing were placed in the center of the table.

"You want another beer?" She walked over to the fridge.

"Nope, I'm good." He never had more than one drink if he was driving. Firm rule. And he was pretty vocal about calling rides for anyone who came to his tavern and overindulged, but all the locals knew that.

They sat across from each other and started their meal. He tried to think of some kind of small talk. He tended bar, for Pete's sake. He was a master at small talk. But for some reason, Beth got him all twisted up and he couldn't think of a darn thing to talk about except for the weather. "I hear we have some cooler weather coming in."

"It has been unseasonably warm for September." She nodded politely.

"Did you have any damage from that late spring storm we got? I lost a tree that fell right across the parking lot at my tavern." More weather talk.

"No, we survived it fine. Though the boys were out at the lodge when it hit. They had a great time sledding and made this huge snow fort. They love it out there."

"Your mom still owns the lodge?" He remembered she'd grown up there. Remembered the hill behind it where she'd fallen down taking a shortcut home...

"Yes, she does. My brother, Jason, works there with her now."

He remembered Jason. Her brother had

been in Mac's grade. Well, the grade Mac finally landed in after they held him back twice.

"Anyway, Jason helps her run the lodge, and I help out in the busy season in the summer when school is out. The boys get to run around the property and I enjoy the work. We have some families that come back year after year. It's like they've become friends now."

He wasn't about to mention that it seemed like her life was pretty full even without adding running for mayor. He'd already made that mistake once.

"Anyway, I've kept you long enough." She stood and gathered her dishes. "Though, I do have ice cream I can offer you for dessert. I always have ice cream. A woman never knows when she might need an emergency bowl of it." She smiled that friendly smile of hers again.

He wanted to just sit and let her smile at him, but that would make him look like some darn fool. He climbed to his feet. "As tempting as that sounds, I should probably head back."

She nodded and took his dishes from his hands.

"You have something to wrap those pieces of the mug in? I'll take it back and see what I can do with it."

She carefully wrapped them in a towel and handed it to him. "Thanks for all your help. I'd never have gotten through all of this without your help."

"You're welcome. It was my pleasure." And it had been. He'd actually enjoyed himself, just spending time with her while they tidied up and the simple, quiet dinner.

She walked him to the front door and he slipped out into the cooling night air. "Well, I'll see you," Beth said.

She stood there staring at him, and he wanted to just turn around and walk back inside. Sit with her. Talk to her. But instead, he just stood there like a fool. He finally said, "Yes, see you. Make sure you lock the door behind me."

"I will."

He turned and walked to his truck, wondering when he'd see her again. At least he had the pieces of the mug. That meant he'd at least see her one more time when he returned it to her.

CHAPTER 10

On Saturday Jason offered to take the boys hiking in the mountains. It was one of those perfect fall days in Colorado. Sunny, warm, and the leaves were just beginning to change to brilliant colors of yellow, orange, and red. The boys were ridiculously excited to be off on their adventure.

Beth stood in the doorway and waved to them as Jason pulled away in his four-wheel-drive. She glanced at the new lock on the door as she headed back inside. Her mother had convinced her to change her locks. She now had strong deadbolts on both the front and back doors with new keys to open them. The very fact she had them seemed wrong to her, but she wasn't going to take any chances with the boys' safety.

In a moment of independence, she left the front door open with just the screen door between her and the outside world. She was tired of having her life tossed upside down by the intruders.

The police had no leads on who might have been involved. Everywhere she went in town, people stopped her and asked her about it. She was ready for the town to move on to some new gossip.

She walked into the kitchen which she'd scrubbed until it was sparkling clean, erasing any trace of whoever had broken in. Her house had never looked so clean. She stood in the kitchen, momentarily lost in the luxury of a day to herself.

She turned and strode over to the pantry and took out the makings for homemade bread. That was one thing she knew how to make and did it well if she did say so herself. On a spur-of-the-moment decision, she decided to make three loaves. One for her and the boys, one for her mother and Jason, and one to bring as a thank-you gift to Mac.

It had nothing to do with the fact that she'd

been trying to come up with an excuse to go see him again. Nothing. She hadn't wanted to just show up and ask about her father's mug. That seemed rude after all he'd done for her.

But a gift?

Yes, that was a great idea.

She started the dough and let it rise. While it sat on the counter rising, she sat at the kitchen table and worked on a presentation she was scheduled to give at the next school board meeting.

After she finished her notes on the presentation, she graded some papers while she baked the bread to a perfect, golden brown. She wrapped a loaf in a clean towel and drove to Mountain Grove to see Mac.

She pulled into the parking lot and headed inside Mac's Tavern. It took a moment for her eyes to adjust from the brightness outside to the low lights inside. As the room came into focus, she saw that almost every patron in the place was staring at her. *Again.*

Fine.

She walked over to the bar, and the bartender came up to her. "What can I get you?"

"I'm looking for Mac."

He stared at her for a moment. "He's upstairs. Through that door and up the stairway in the back."

On the first floor, she found a storage room with kegs of beer, boxes of liquor, and cases of soda all stacked neatly in columns. Almost as spotless as his truck. The stairs creaked beneath her as she headed up the first flight. More storage on this floor. How many floors of storage did a tavern need?

She headed up the next flight of stairs. At the top of the stairs, there was a small landing and a door. Taking a deep breath, she rapped sharply on the door.

"Come in." Mac's voice drifted out into the hallway.

She turned the knob and pushed the door open. Her surprise was only outdone by Mac's. She stood in the entrance of a huge loft with exposed brick walls and a high, pine ceiling. Her eyes glanced over to the couch, TV, and stereo situated in one area. His bed was tucked into the far corner. He stood in the kitchen area tossing a salad. With no shirt on and looking… looking just fine.

The bartender could have told her Mac *lived* here for Pete's sake.

"Beth, what are you doing here?" He walked over to a chair and snatched a shirt off the back of it and shrugged it on, covering his strong shoulders and hardened abs, not that she'd noticed.

"I—I brought you a thank-you present for all you did." She held out the loaf, suddenly feeling like she was intruding. "Homemade bread."

"You didn't have to do that. But thank you." He reached for it and walked back to the kitchen area. "Uh… come in, I guess."

Even though he didn't sound very certain of his invitation, she entered his home. She walked farther into the loft, taking in the photos covering one wall. A view of the mountains taken in each of the four seasons. A closeup of a columbine. A crisp black and white photo of a mountain river threading its way through a grove of pine trees.

"I was just getting ready to eat. I made some homemade soup. I was going to have a salad with it. Would you like to stay and eat with me?"

She paused and looked at her watch. She had time. "That sounds wonderful."

He nodded over to the couch. "Make yourself comfortable while I finish up."

She slipped out of her coat and hung it on a hook beside Mac's jacket by the door. She crossed the room and browsed through the bookshelves, wondering what type of books interested him. He had a whole wall of bookshelves.

She felt him watching her as she read through the titles. Everything from the history of Australia to zoo animals. A lot of them were books on tape. Boxed tapes in their original boxes or put into plastic snap containers, neatly labeled with title and author. Discs in their sleeves. Quite a few of them had the paper version of the book slipped in beside them.

The books appeared to be arranged precisely. Nonfiction by subject. Fiction by author.

"Find anything interesting?" His voice floated across the room.

"Actually, yes. You've got quite a collection of books here."

"Aren't you going to ask why so many of them are audio books?"

"I figured you'd rather listen to them than read them." She crossed over to the kitchen area and watched him take an extended swallow of a long-necked beer.

"I'll have one of those if you have another one." She motioned to the beer.

He walked to the refrigerator and pulled out another one. He popped the top off, set it on the counter, and motioned to a barstool. "Here, sit down."

MAC WATCHED her take a long swallow of beer then brush her lips with the back of her hand. Her fingers were long and slender. He'd never seen such delicate hands. Oh, he probably had, but her hands fascinated him. Carefully polished nails in a subdued color. Watching her paint her nails might be as interesting as watching her put on her makeup in his truck the night he'd rescued her. That had fascinated him, too.

He pushed those thoughts aside and scooped up big bowls of soup and plates of salad and set them on the counter. He sliced the bread and grabbed some butter from the fridge.

He crossed around the counter, and his knee brushed her thigh as he slid onto the stool beside her. She jerked her leg away and concentrated on her salad.

They ate in silence, but he could feel the

tension charged between them. His thoughts drifted to memories of their school days together. Memories he had deliberately pushed to the back of his mind, that were fighting desperately to come to the forefront now.

She finally broke the quiet. "The books on tape—the audiobooks. I've never seen anyone own so many. You like listening to books rather than reading them?"

"I can read if that's what you're asking." He knew his voice sounded defensive, but this was such a touchy subject for him.

"I wasn't questioning your reading ability. I've just never seen someone own so many."

"I didn't mean to jump at you. I guess old habits die hard. I was so used to being teased about my reading. You've brought back a lot of memories from my school days."

Her warm brown eyes looked directly at him. "They did give you a hard time at school, didn't they?"

"I wasn't looking for your sympathy." He knew his voice sounded tight again. He let out a long, drawn-out breath. "I'm sorry." He reached up and raked his fingers through his hair. "I try not to think about my days at school. Anyway, things turned out fine for me. I have this bar. I enjoy running it." He wasn't sure why he wanted to impress her and assure her he was doing fine now.

"School can be a rough time for some kids. Especially for troublemakers."

He looked up quickly and saw her grinning at him. "I guess I got into my share of trouble."

"I guess you did."

"Mostly I just wanted to be left alone." He paused and looked over at her sitting perched on a barstool sipping beer from the long-necked bottle. In his apartment. Who would have ever thought?

He felt an easiness drift in between them now. Like bringing the past up had somehow broken the tension between them.

Not sure why he felt compelled to explain it to her, he nevertheless continued. "I found out after I left high school that I had a learning disability. It was never diagnosed in school, so everyone thought I was dumb. Including me." He twisted sideways on the stool to face her.

"The guy who owned this bar, JT, took me under his wing after I dropped out of high school. He read everything he could get his hands on. He came across some books on learning disabilities and figured out that was my problem. He even paid for me to go to a special tutor who taught me how to read. I just hadn't been able to learn reading in the normal ways they teach kids. I finally got my GED and even took some classes at the college here in town."

"Learning disabilities. Of course. That explains so much. You seemed so bright, yet you never seemed to do anything with it." Beth shook her head. "I should have guessed."

"Well, it wasn't something people really looked for back then. And once I started getting into trouble, they used that as an excuse."

"They still don't do much for the learning disabled at the school. I'm actually giving a presentation to the school board, asking for funds for a new program to help them."

"Good luck with that. The people on the school board don't impress me as very progressive. When I was there, they seemed to like the average kids."

"We do have some special education provided by the state. But there is so much more we could do with the kids' different learning styles. It would benefit all the children. Some kids learn better by listening. Other kids need to see things to learn. Some kids need to touch, to feel, to grasp things in a concrete way."

"Well, good luck. I can't see that this town is up for many changes. Some of those teachers have been there since Adam and Eve. Teaching the same lesson plan, in the same way, each year."

Beth sighed. "I know it will be a battle. Change is always a battle in Sweet River Falls."

"You sure have a lot of battles ahead of you. This one. Running for mayor."

"Sophie says I'm always on a crusade. Maybe I am." She shrugged. "I just like… well, I like to help people and get involved in things that help the town."

Beth Cassidy was a remarkable woman. And she was sitting here. With him.

He couldn't quite get his head wrapped around that fact.

"So, this JT helped you, then you took over his bar and named it Mac's place?"

"Actually, no. His name is JT MacDonald. Everyone called him Mac, so he named it Mac's Place. Worked for me, too." He grinned.

"I guess it did." She gave him a small smile in return.

He so enjoyed that smile of hers…

"Anyway, JT retired and moved to Florida. I bought the tavern from him. Miss having him around, though. He was a good friend to me." JT had actually been the first friend Mac had ever had, even with their differences in age. He did miss that. A lot. But JT had wanted to move to a warmer climate when he retired, so off to Florida he'd gone.

Beth stood and neatly placed her napkin beside her plate. "Well, I should go. Jason has the boys, and they'll probably be back soon. Thank you for the meal. It was great. The soup was wonderful."

"You're welcome." She was welcome any time she wanted to come. *Anytime.* "Here, I'll show you out."

She walked to the door, and he reached for her jacket and helped her slip it on. He settled it gently on her shoulders, and she gave him that small smile of hers again.

"Thanks again."

And just like that she turned and slipped out the door, leaving emptiness cascading through the loft.

CHAPTER 11

The next day Mac realized he hadn't given Beth back the mug he'd fixed when she'd come by his loft. He'd done a pretty good job with the repair. He'd painstakingly pieced it together and filled in one small missing spot. It probably wouldn't hold hot liquid again, but maybe she could fill it with pens, or a plant, or something that would make her happy. He was ridiculously pleased with the thought of making Beth happy.

Which was silly, because, really? How long had she been back in his life? A week, maybe less?

Even though it was a crazy idea, he decided to head to Sweet River Falls and return the mug.

It was the *friendly* thing to do, right? Besides, he hadn't been able to get the thought of her out of his mind since she'd left yesterday.

Before long he'd pulled into Beth's drive. Her mother's car sat in the driveway, a complication he hadn't counted on. He deliberated on just pulling the truck back out of the drive and heading home. He didn't want to intrude, and Beth sure didn't seem eager to be seen with him or introduce him to her family. Before he could make up his mind, Beth's mother came out on the front porch. She waved to him and motioned for him to come.

No turning back now.

He climbed out of his truck, cautiously holding the small box where he'd carefully placed the restored mug.

"It's Mac McKenna, right?" Beth's mother held out a hand.

He took her hand, careful to keep his grip on the box with his other hand. Her firm handshake surprised him. "Yes, ma'am."

"Nora. I'm Nora. Come on in. Beth is out back with the boys. I saw you pull up."

He followed the woman through the house and out the back door.

"Beth, you have a visitor."

Beth looked up from a game of catch with the boys. A smile crossed her face, rewarding him with the rightness of his choice to come visit. The two boys stopped playing and stared at him. He crossed over to where they were standing out in the yard.

"Trevor, Connor, this is Mr. McKenna."

"Hi." The two boys said it in unison.

"Hi, boys. Connor." He pointed to the oldest boy. "And Trevor, right?" He added, pointing to the younger boy.

"Yep, you got it right." Connor nodded.

"Wanna see our tree house?" Trevor walked up to him, his bright blue eyes shining.

"Sure do, just a sec." He turned to Beth. "I brought you this."

She reached for the small box and slowly opened it, unwrapping it from the layers of tissue paper he'd carefully placed around it. "Oh, it looks almost like new. Thank you."

Nora walked up beside him. "Is that your father's mug?"

"Yes, it got broken when—" Beth looked at the boys. "A little bit ago."

"Well, it looks like it's all back together now."

"Thank you, Mac. That was so nice of

you." Beth smiled at him, and a feeling of success washed over him. He did so like making her smile.

"That was really nice of you, Mr. McKenna." Nora smiled at him too, and he was startled at how alike Beth and her mother looked.

"Mac. Please. Call me Mac."

"Mac it is." Nora nodded.

"Ya coming, Mr. McKenna?" Trevor called out from near the tree house.

"I'm coming." He headed over to the boys.

"This is our tree house. It's great, huh? Only this board keeps falling off. And that one is broken." Trevor pointed to a board on the side, hanging by one loose nail, and another split board.

"I bet we could fix that."

"Really?"

"You think your mom has a hammer and some nails?"

"I bet so." Connor took off at a run. "Hey, Mom. Mr. McKenna is going to help us fix those loose boards on the tree house."

Within minutes, Connor came back with a hammer and nails, and Mac started helping the boys repair their tree house.

He'd never had a tree house, and the structure fascinated him. He could only imagine having a place like this as a child. A place to escape to, to hide out in. These boys were very lucky kids.

NORA WATCHED as Mac helped the boys repair their tree house. He carefully explained safety with a hammer, then let each boy have a try nailing in the boards.

"He's good with them." She set down the small trowel she was using to plant some bulbs in a flowerbed in the backyard.

Beth grabbed a sack of bulb food and sprinkled some in the holes her mother had dug. She glanced over at the boys. "He's very patient with them, isn't he?"

"He seems like a nice young man." Nora dropped a bulb into the hole and gently covered it with soil.

"You're probably the first person in Sweet River Falls to ever say that about him." Beth watched while Mac climbed into the tree house with the boys.

"I remember he had quite a reputation

when you were in school." Nora plopped another bulb in the ground.

"He did. But you know what I found out? He had undiagnosed learning disabilities. He must have struggled so hard to try and keep up and fit in. It's a shame, really. Our school system should do so much more."

"Maybe your presentation to the school board will help."

"I sure hope so. The state does some, but we could do so much more. These learning-disabled kids are getting lost in the shuffle. Jenny Larson's son was teased for years until they figured out he had a reading disability. Kids can be mean. Anyway, he got some help through the state special education program, but it wasn't enough. If Jenny hadn't been able to afford a tutor, he'd never have caught up with his grade level."

"What about the kids who parents can't afford a private tutor?" Nora pushed a lock of hair out of her face with the back of her hand.

"I know." Beth sighed. "And you know how this school is. They like the middle of the road kids. Average. Not exceptionally bright, nor ones with any disability. Both ends of the spectrum get left out. I want that to change."

Nora could hear the urgency in her daughter's voice. "I'm sure you'll do your best to see if you can make that happen."

Truth be told, Nora was beginning to worry about Beth. She had the boys, her teaching job, this crusade to help the kids at her school who needed extra help... and now this mayor's race. Mayor of Sweet River Falls wasn't a full-time position, but it would take up a lot of Beth's time.

There didn't seem like there would be enough hours in the day for all of that. Well, she'd help Beth as much as she could. She loved having the boys around. She could help out with that. But Beth was going to have to figure out how to sort out all the rest of it.

Trevor came racing back to where she and Beth were planting the bulbs.

"Can I help?" He dropped to his knees beside her.

"Of course." Nora handed him a bulb and explained to him how to plant it correctly.

His face screwed up in concentration as he carefully placed the bulb and covered it. "Like that, Grams?"

"Just like that."

Mac and Connor crossed the yard and stood

watching. Mac handed the hammer and extra nails to Connor. "Can you put these back where you got them? Always put your tools away when you're finished so you can find them again easily."

"Okay." Connor took the tools and headed for the garage.

"Do you need some help with the planting?" Mac asked.

"No, we're about done. I'll let the boys help me finish up." Once again Nora thought that Mac McKenna was a polite young man.

"I guess I'll be going, then."

Mac didn't seem very eager to leave. Nora liked that. "Beth, why don't you walk Mac out?"

Beth stood and brushed the dirt off of her jeans. "Thanks for helping the boys with the tree house."

"No problem."

"And thank you so much for fixing my father's mug. It means a lot to me."

"Really, it wasn't a big deal." A hint of an embarrassed blush crossed Mac's face.

Nora could see he was a man not used to compliments or thanks.

"It was a big deal to me." Beth started into the house, and Mac followed her.

He turned when he got to the doorway. "Bye, Trevor."

"Bye, Mr. McKenna. You should come back and play with us again soon." Trevor looked up at Mac.

Nora could see the look in Trevor's eyes. Mac was already a friend as far as Trevor was concerned.

Connor walked around the corner from the garage and up to Mac. "Bye, Mr. McKenna. Thanks for the help."

"My pleasure." Mac disappeared inside the house.

Nora went back to planting the bulbs with the boys, hoping to keep them entertained long enough to give Beth and Mac some privacy. Mac was the first man she'd seen her daughter show the tiniest bit of interest in since her divorce from Scott. She was certainly not going to be the person to stand in their way. She'd even like to give them a little push if she could think up a reason to get them back together again...

MAC STOOD on the front step with Beth by his

side. He had to keep himself from reaching out and brushing away a streak of dirt from her reddened cheek. He didn't think she'd be very receptive to his touch.

Too forward.

But he wanted to.

As if she could read his thoughts, she reached up and wiped at her cheek with her sleeve.

"Well… thank you for the mug and for everything."

"Sure." He desperately struggled to think of something else to say. Some way to continue to spend more moments with her. He'd been so disappointed when Beth's mother had turned down his offer to help plant the bulbs.

He turned at the sound of the screen door opening behind him.

Nora peeked her head out the door. "So the boys and I decided they should come over to the lodge and have dinner with me later. We're going to make homemade pizza. How about I have Miss Judy make you two a picnic basket and you could picnic by the lake? Beth could use the break. She works too hard."

"Mom, I'm sure Mr. McKenna has better things to do with his evening."

Oh, no he didn't. "Actually... I can't think of a better way to spend my evening."

"You sure?" Beth looked uncertain.

"I'm sure."

"Great. Come over about five. Beth will be wanting to get the boys back home before too late since it's a school night. But that should give you two time for a nice, relaxing meal. Nothing better than a nice picnic outside by the lake. Might as well take advantage of this weather before it turns too cold."

"I appreciate the invite." He turned and hurried to the truck, glancing at his watch. If he hurried, he'd just have time to head back to Mountain Grove, check on things at the tavern, and put on a clean shirt. He wondered if Beth considered this a date with him?

Or... what was it, really?

Whatever it was, he was pleased to be seeing her again tonight. He climbed into the truck and waved to Beth and her mother as he pulled out of the driveway.

So far this day had turned out way better than he'd expected.

∾

"MOM, WHAT ARE YOU DOING?" Beth turned to her mother as Mac pulled out of the drive.

"What do you mean?" Her mother feigned innocence, but Beth was having none of it.

"Why did you invite him over? It's almost like you set us up on a *date*."

"Call it what you want. Personally, I'd simply call it a picnic." Nora turned and headed into the house. She called back over her shoulder. "I'm going to go ahead and take the boys to the lodge with me. You can get cleaned up. You have a smudge of dirt on your face, by the way."

Beth walked to the mirror hanging over a small table by the door and scrubbed at her face with her hand. Large wisps of hair had broken free of her french braid. She looked a mess. What a great impression she must have made on Mac.

Immediately she was annoyed that she even *cared* what kind of impression she made on him.

She headed to her room to clean up, but only because she didn't want to look like such a wreck. Only because a woman had a sense of pride in her looks, not because she cared about Mac's opinion.

A shower and three changes of clothes later, she headed over to the lodge.

CHAPTER 12

Beth shook out the blanket and set it on the ground by the lake. The early evening rays of sun filtered through the tree branches, tossing spots of light on the blanket.

"Here, let me help with that." Mac straightened out the blanket and set the picnic basket at the edge.

Beth knelt on the blanket and began to unpack the basket. Miss Judy had put in chicken salad sandwiches, chips, fruit slices and a couple of huge pieces of chocolate cake. "Well, this is enough to feed an army."

"Good, I'm starving." Mac tossed a lazy grin at her.

She tried not to let him see the effect his smile had on her. She picked up a sandwich and promptly dropped it. She picked it up again and carefully unwrapped it. She handed it to him and he took a bite. She tried not to stare at him while he gazed out at the lake and enjoyed his supper. The golden light bathed his strong cheekbones. He looked over at her, and she quickly concentrated on her own sandwich.

"It's really quiet and peaceful here, isn't it?" He motioned toward the lake.

"It is. I really love it here. Though there are rumors that Dobbs is trying to get the zoning here changed. He wants to sell some land he owns on the far side of the lake to a condo developer."

"He can't do that, can he?"

"Not if I have anything to say about it. There are plenty of lakes in Colorado with condos and motorboats and noise. Lone Elk Lake is just so... well, like you said, peaceful."

"It would be a shame to ruin all this." He looked out over the lake. "A real shame."

"Well, I'm going to do everything I can to make sure it doesn't happen."

"Dobbs is a hard one to fight, I'd imagine."

"He is, but no way is he going to ruin this lake. Not only because it would hurt Mom's business, but because... well, I love this lake. I grew up here. So many people come to enjoy the serenity here. There's a small park at the far end of the lake with picnic tables, a gazebo, and a fishing dock. It's just... lots of people come here to enjoy it. I'd hate to see condos and motorboats come in.

"Well, I hope none of that happens. I hope it all can stay the same. I'm all for needed change. Everything eventually changes, doesn't it? But I don't see the need for ruining the tranquility of this place." He shook his head.

They sat in quiet for a while, finishing up their dinner. The sky began to burst forth in streaks of yellow and orange slashing through the white fluffy clouds.

"It's going to be a gorgeous sunset." She reached for the chocolate cake and handed Mac a piece.

"Looks like it. I'm usually busy working this time of night and don't get to see too many sunsets."

"This is my favorite spot to watch them."

Mac took a bite of the cake. "Mm, this is good."

"Miss Judy makes the best chocolate cake."

"I'd have to say I agree with you."

Silence drifted around them again as they

sat and watched the sunset deepen. A peace settled over Beth. It was nice to slow down and just enjoy the moment. She didn't do that very often, and she should.

MAC GLANCED OVER AT BETH, her face bathed in the golden light of the sunset. He'd love to just freeze this moment in time and take it out again and again to enjoy it like a person did with a beloved photograph. Just being with her like this felt so right... and so strange at the same time.

He reached over with a napkin. "You got a spot of chocolate here in the corner of your mouth." He gently wiped it away.

She self-consciously swiped at her mouth with the back of her hand.

"No, I got it all." He smiled at her, and she rewarded him with her warm smile in return.

A crazy thought flashed through his brain.

He'd really like to lean over and kiss her.

Before he had a chance to act on his impulse, she picked up her plate and dropped it into the picnic basket. "I guess we should pack this up. I really do need to go round up the boys and get them home."

He reluctantly got to his feet, the opportunity for a kiss broken in an instant of indecision. He reached down his hands for her. She put her hands in his, and a shock of electric connection flashed through him. Her warm hands grasped his as he effortlessly helped her to her feet. As she rose, she started to lose her balance and fell against him, banging into his chest.

He tightened an arm around her. "You okay?"

That smile again. "I'm fine."

He reluctantly lessened his hold on her. They picked up the remnants of their picnic and put them back in the basket. He grabbed the basket and they headed back toward Nora's cabin.

Their hands brushed once as they started along the path. He debated taking her hand in his.

Once again, his indecision cost him his moment.

Beth paused and turned back to get one more look at the sunset.

He watched her look at the view, a sweet

smile of contentment resting on her face.

Yet another moment he'd like to freeze in time.

BETH TOOK the picnic basket from Mac as they reached her mother's cabin. "Thank you. I had a really good time. I think I just needed the break."

"I'm glad you enjoyed yourself. I did too." Mac looked as if he was going to say something else, but he didn't.

"Well, I better round up the boys."

"Beth... I... um. Would you like to go out to eat?" He shuffled his feet. "Not tonight, of course. I mean another night. With me. Maybe tomorrow?" He let out a long breath of air, then tossed her a shy grin. "I'm not very good at this, am I?"

"So, you're asking me out on a date?" Her mind reeled. She didn't really want to date anyone. Especially now. Things were just crazy in her life. And yet she'd had a wonderful time with Mac tonight. Her thoughts bounced like a rock skipped across the lake.

"I wasn't very clear, was I?" He shook his

head, a mild look of disgust covering his face. "Yes, would you like to go out with me?"

"Well, I can't tomorrow. I have to stay late and work with one of my students. He has learning disabilities and I'm trying so hard to unlock things for him. Find a way to get things into his brain. He's trying hard, too."

"I could help you with that."

"What?"

"Like, you know, a volunteer or something. Seriously, I know a lot about teaching people with learning disabilities. Once I unlocked the secret to reading for me, I did a ton of research. I keep up with new techniques. Maybe I could help him. I'd love to pay it forward for all that JT did for me when he taught me to read."

"Are you sure?"

"I'm positive. Why don't you let me come by after school tomorrow? I'll bring some books I have. Let me work with him."

"That would be great. I'll check with his mom to make sure it's okay with her, but I'm sure it will be."

"Then I'll see you after school tomorrow."

"I'll see you then."

He turned and headed to his truck, a soft whistle trailing behind him as he walked away.

CHAPTER 13

Mac pulled into the school parking lot right as school let out the next day. Kids streamed out of the building to waiting buses and cars. He waited until some of the chaos settled down, then climbed out of his truck, a stack of books tucked under his arm.

He pushed through the front door and saw the large sign. "Please check in at the front office." He swallowed. He could do that. It made sense in this day and age to have visitors check in. He strode to the office, trying to feel like he belonged, and pushed the door open.

A lady at the desk smiled at him. "May I help you?"

"I'm here as a volunteer. Beth Cassidy is expecting me."

The lady walked behind her desk, contacted Beth, and turned back toward him. "Yes, she's expecting you. Here's your visitor badge."

He pinned a badge onto his shirt and headed down the hallway, trying not to let the rows of lockers and endless floor tile intimidate him.

A grown man.

Intimidated by a school.

Beth stood in the doorway of her class as if waiting to rescue him from the torment of his memories. "Hi."

"Hi." He peeked around her to see a young boy sitting at a desk.

"That's Jimmy Nelson. Come, let me introduce you."

He followed her into the room.

"Jimmy, this is Mr. McKenna. Mac, this is Jimmy Nelson."

"Miss Cassidy says you're like me." The boy looked up at him.

"Well, I like to think that everyone is different in their own way. But, yes, my brain kind of works like yours. We think and learn things differently than others. Not wrong. Just different." Mac slipped onto a low chair beside the boy, maneuvering to find room to stretch his legs out.

"Well, I hate it. I just want to be like everyone else."

He remembered feeling just like Jimmy Nelson. It was hard trying to fit in and trying to read and keep up with your classmates. "You don't need to be like them. You can be like you. We'll find a way to sort through all this. We'll get you reading. Let's see if we can work together to make that happen. I'm not saying it will be easy, but we'll work at it together. Deal?"

"Deal." Jimmy nodded his head enthusiastically.

Mac spread out some books on the table. "Let's get started."

"I'll just be over at my desk grading papers. You two do your thing." Beth turned and walked away.

BETH TRIED NOT to make it obvious that she was watching Mac and Jimmy. Mac actually had the boy laughing at one point. They both sat with their heads bent over the material Mac had brought with him.

Mac McKenna was such a complicated mix of a man. Business owner. Patient teacher to Jimmy. Confident, but at times she saw the tiniest hint of insecurity. Strong, but gentle and just a bit rough around the edges.

She bowed her head over her papers and tried to pretend she was grading them. But, mostly, she was watching Mac.

An hour later, Sheila Nelson showed up at the doorway to the class. She walked over to Beth's desk. "Is that Jimmy smiling?"

"It is." Beth stood. "He and Mr. McKenna seem to have hit it off."

Mac glanced their direction and flashed a just a minute sign. They finished up and Jimmy raced up to his mother. "Mom, look. Mr. McKenna said I could bring this home tonight. I read a bunch of pages in the book." He opened the book. "See how this word looks like a bed. Bed. Look at the outline of the word. It even looks like a bed with a headboard and footboard. He taught me some other tricks, too."

Sheila reached out to Mac. "Mr. McKenna, thank you so much for working with Jimmy."

"It's not a problem. I hope we can make things easier for him. Teach him how to read and some coping skills for organization and whatever else I can help him with."

"Come on, Mom." Jimmy tugged on Sheila's hand. "You said we could go to Bookish Cafe and get some ice cream after my lesson. I'm gonna show this book to Miss Annie."

Sheila and Jimmy walked out of the classroom, and Beth leaned against the edge of her desk. "You were really good with him."

"It's obvious he's a sharp kid and anxious to learn. He'll do fine. We just have to figure out the best way to unlock his brain and get the information in there."

"He's usually so stressed by the end of the lesson when I'm working with him, but you sent him out of here in smiles."

"Sometimes it helps just to know there's someone like you who understands." Mac lounged against her desk beside her.

Inches from her. Not that she noticed. Their fingers almost touched. She might be imagining it, but she'd swear she could feel the heat of his skin jump the distance between them.

He cleared his throat. "So, I left last night without getting an answer."

"To what?" She knew darn well what he meant.

"I asked if you wanted to go out on a date with me." His eyes flashed with determination.

There was no way he was going to let the question go this time, she could see that.

"I… it's complicated. I have the boys, the job, running for mayor. My life is just so crazy right now." She was actually late to pick the boys up from her mother's right now. Her life *was* busy and crazy… it *wasn't* just an excuse.

"So, you don't want to date me?" He asked her point blank.

"It's not that. I just don't have time to be involved with anyone right now."

"I wasn't asking for a long commitment or anything, just a simple date. But I understand."

She could see the hurt in his eyes. A hurt that he tried so hard to hide from her.

"Mac, I—"

"Hey, it's no problem." He pushed off the desk and headed for the door. He turned when he got to the door. "When is Jimmy supposed to have another session?"

"Thursday."

"I'll be here."

Without another word, he disappeared out into the hall. The complete and utter silence of her classroom was broken only by the tick-tock-tick of the clock on the wall.

BETH WALKED into the cheery warmth of her mother's cabin. "Hey, boys. I'm here. Time to go home."

"Mom, I'm almost finished with my homework. Uncle Jason helped me." Trevor called out.

She walked into the kitchen where her mother stood at the stove. "I've made some homemade soup. I was going to send some home with you for dinner."

"That would be great, Mom." She sank into a kitchen chair. Now she didn't have to face that daily question of what to fix the boys for dinner.

Her mother turned to her. "Do you remember that nice young couple from Florida who got stuck here in the big snow storm last spring? The boys befriended their son, Tommy."

"I remember. The boys were fascinated by someone who lived right by the beach. They've never even seen the ocean. I should take them sometime…" She'd just put that on her ever-growing to-do list. Sometimes it seemed like that there just wasn't enough time to do everything she wanted to do.

"Well, I think they're going to become some more of our repeat customers. People sure do come here and fall in love with the place."

"*If* we can keep the lake like it is." Beth sighed. They were going to have a long fight ahead of them.

"Hey, sis." Jason came around the corner and swiped a piece of cornbread her mom had cooling on a rack by the stove. "The boys are almost finished."

"Thanks for helping them with their homework." That was another chore she wouldn't have tonight. The ever-present homework battle.

"I don't mind at all." He reached for another piece of cornbread.

"Before you eat all that, how about grabbing a container and packing some up for your sister and the boys." Her mom waved a spoon at Jason.

He went to the cabinet and took out a container and filled it with cornbread. "I heard you're seeing Mac McKenna."

"I'm not really *seeing* him."

"Right. You just had a picnic with him here at the lake. And the boys have met him. Heard he dropped by your house. He helped with their tree house. And Mom said he helped clean up your house after the break-in. Yep, sounds like just normal, everyday, not-seeing-each-other to me." Jason's eyes sparkled.

"Jason, quit teasing your sister and get me a container for the soup."

"He's just a friend."

"I see." Jason rolled his eyes. "Rescued you from your flat tire calamity, too."

"Are you keeping score?"

"Pretty much." Jason nodded agreeably.

"I think it's time for me to go." Beth stood, and her mom handed her a box with the food containers.

"There are cookies in there, too."

"Thanks, Mom." She leaned through the doorway and called to the boys, "Let's go."

"Coming." She heard the scraping of chairs and the commotion of them gathering their things.

They entered the kitchen and hugged her mom. "Bye, Grams."

"Bye, Uncle Jason." Trevor slipped on his jacket.

"Bye, boys." Jason swiped yet another piece of cornbread.

Beth swore the man never stopped eating. Or stopped teasing her.

The boys raced out the door.

"Have fun *not* seeing your Mac McKenna."

"He's not *my*..."

Jason grinned at her. She grabbed a kitchen towel and swatted at him.

"Hey, you two are too old for that nonsense." But her mother smiled in spite of herself.

"Okay, I'm outta here." Beth put down the towel, left the warmth of her mother's home, and headed out into the chilly Colorado evening.

CHAPTER 14

Mac had been meeting with Jimmy twice a week for a few weeks now. He and Beth had gotten into the habit of sitting and talking after Jimmy left. He'd come to look forward to those late afternoons with her.

He'd made up an excuse today to come by the school even though it wasn't a regular lesson time with Jimmy. His excuse, a printout of a new research project on techniques to teach kids with dyslexia, sat on the front seat of his truck. He knew she'd enjoy reading the article.

And he'd enjoy seeing her...

He spied her car at the far end of the parking lot and slowly drove the truck over. He parked beside it, trying to decide if he should wait outside for her or work up the courage to actually go into the school and look for her. After all these weeks, he still wasn't comfortable entering the silly school. Which was ridiculous. He was a grown man. He shouldn't be afraid of a school building.

He climbed out of the truck. As he passed the driver's side of Beth's car, he paused and frowned. With a quick glance around the lot, he walked over closer and bent down. Her front tire was low, and someone or something had punctured it, maybe with a knife. He ran his finger over the puncture.

As he stood up and looked around again, a police car with flashing lights pulled into the parking lot and stopped behind Beth's car, blocking him in.

"Stay where you are." Daniel Smith stepped out of the car.

"What's the problem?"

"That's what I'm here to figure out. I got a call that someone was out lurking around the cars in the lot."

"Yes, it appears that Beth's car might have been tampered with." Mac tried to steady his pounding heart, annoyed that he was having this reaction. *He* hadn't done anything.

"And you just happen to be here by her car?"

"I was coming to… I have something for her. I noticed the flat and was checking on it."

"Awful lot of coincidences there, don't you think?" Daniel's partner came to stand by his side.

The two of them stared at Mac. "Why don't you put your hands against the car?"

"You're kidding me." Mac gave both of them one long look, then placed his hands against Beth's car.

"Got any weapons on you?"

"Of course not."

Mac gritted his teeth as Daniel ran his hands over him, searching, patting him down.

"What's this?" Daniel held up a knife.

"That…" Mac looked at what Daniel was holding, and his heart thudded in his chest. "That's my knife. I was using it to open boxes at my tavern. Didn't realize I still had it in my pocket."

Daniel's partner bent down and looked at Beth's tire. "Looks like it's been punctured with a knife."

"I didn't puncture Beth's tire," Mac said slowly and forcefully.

This school held some kind of curse over him. He was always being accused of wrongdoing. Even after all these years.

"What's going on here?"

Mac looked up to see Beth standing near her car. A brief flash of embarrassment stabbed through him at her seeing him standing here, legs spread, hands on her car.

"Caught him messing with your tire." Daniel held the knife flat in his palm. "Caught him red-handed."

"I don't understand." Beth's eyes clouded with confusion.

"We got a call that someone was lurking around the cars on the lot. We pulled up and Mr. McKenna was bending over by your tire. Found this knife on him."

"Mac?" She turned to look at him.

"Didn't do it." He looked at her. "I was coming to see you and noticed your tire was flat."

Beth stared at him, then looked at Daniel.

He waited what seemed like an eternity for her to say something.

"If Mac says that's what happened, then it is."

"But we caught him." Daniel's partner insisted.

"You actually saw him puncture the tire?" She walked up beside Mac and rested her hand over one of his pressed against her car.

"Well… not exactly. But he was here and has the knife and he was kneeling by the tire." Daniel frowned.

"He said he was checking it."

Daniel nodded at Mac. "You can stand up."

Mac slowly stood up straight, anger mixed in with embarrassment flooding through him. He balled his hands into fists, but then relaxed them and jammed them in his pockets.

"I'd still like to run him in for questioning." Daniel turned to Beth.

"I'm not going to press charges against him."

He felt Beth standing just inches by his side.

"I think you're making a mistake." Daniel's partner insisted.

"I don't think I am." Beth stood firm.

Charlie Patterson—Mac could finally read the name on his badge. He'd add that name to the list of people to avoid in this town.

"Okay. Your choice. You need help changing that flat tire?" Daniel offered.

"I'll change it for her." Mac stood beside Beth, every muscle in his body screaming at him, trying to hold back all the emotions that plagued him. Anger. Embarrassment. Protectiveness toward Beth. And last, but not least, an intense dislike that he had for this school and everything associated with it.

Good old Charlie looked distrusting and doubtful.

"Thank you, Mac. I'd appreciate that." Beth stood by his side in what he couldn't help but feel was solidarity. He wanted to throw his arms around her and hug her but figured that wasn't the appropriate move at this time.

Daniel nodded, and he and Charlie headed back to their vehicle. Beth didn't move or say a word until they pulled out of the lot.

He sucked in a deep breath, struggling to steady his nerves.

She turned to him and looked at him with her warm brown eyes. "You didn't do this, did you?"

She might as well have taken his knife and stabbed his heart.

～

BETH LOOKED deep into Mac's eyes. She couldn't help it. She needed to look straight at him and watch his face and his eyes when he answered her question. She had to know the truth. *Feel* the truth. She didn't think he did it, but he did have a way of showing up when these things happened.

He didn't answer her for a full minute. He just stood there staring at her. "I can't believe you're asking me that." He jammed his hands into his jeans pockets. "No, I did not puncture your tire. It wasn't me."

"I'm sorry… I just…" How did she explain that she had to ask him again? Had to ask when Daniel and Charlie weren't around. When she could watch his face when he answered. She had her boys to consider. She had to be careful, for their sake, if not for her own.

She could read the expression on his face clearly now. He was hurt. Disappointed. Maybe even angry.

He turned away from her. "Open your trunk. I'll get your tire changed and then I'll get out of your way."

"Mac… I…"

"No problem." He stood by the trunk.

She opened it, and he wrestled the spare

out. He didn't say one word to her while he changed her tire.

When he finished changing the tire and putting the punctured one into the trunk, he stood and wiped his hands on his jeans. Dirt covered the knees of his jeans where he'd knelt to change the tire.

"I'll be going now." He turned away from her and took a step toward his truck.

She reached out and grabbed his arm. "Mac—"

"Save it. I'll never outrun my reputation in this town. Ever. I'm through trying to persuade people in Sweet River Falls that I'm not some big troublemaker or, apparently at this stage, a criminal."

"Mac, I don't think—"

"Frankly, I don't care what you think." He pulled away from her grasp and climbed into his truck.

She watched as he pulled out of the parking lot and headed down the road, wondering if that was the last time she'd ever see him.

CHAPTER 15

Beth sat at Bookish Cafe sipping coffee with Sophie. "I really messed up. Mac doesn't want anything to do with me."

"And that's a problem, isn't it? Because you're falling for him?" Sophie eyed her over the rim of her mug.

"What? No, of course not." She frowned. She wasn't exactly falling for the man... She just... liked him. He was fun to be around. She enjoyed their time together. That was all.

Sophie rolled her eyes. "I've known you too long. Good try with the denial." She tilted her head. "Though, maybe you're just trying to convince yourself there's nothing there."

"I... well, I think I hurt his feelings when I asked him if he slit my tire. But I mean, why did

I ask him? What reason would he have to do that? It was a silly question, and I just convinced myself that I had to watch his expression when I asked him, so I knew the truth."

"And what did his expression say?"

"That he was hurt that I'd asked him. And I think he was embarrassed to be seen like that. Hands against my car." She pushed a lock of hair away from her face. "He'd also asked me out to dinner, and I turned him down. I was busy that night, but honestly, my life is so crazy right now. Why would I add in one more thing?"

"Because you like this guy?"

"I don't like him. Well, I like him. I just don't *like-like* him. Oh, you know what I mean."

"Actually, I do know what you mean. You like him a lot. You just won't admit it."

Beth stared at her friend. Her friend who was telling the truth even if she hadn't seen it. She *did* like him.

"I kind of understand why you asked him about the tire. Maybe. But why would he puncture your tire? It makes no sense. He has been around when a lot of things have happened, but I just don't get the feeling any of that involves him. He seems like a fine, upstanding guy. And he was there helping Jimmy Nelson. I really think he's a nice guy." Sophie set down her mug.

"I don't know how to make it right with him now."

"I've got an idea." Sophie grinned.

Beth wasn't sure she liked that grin on her friend's face. "What is it?"

"Go to Mac's Place and apologize."

"If he would even listen to me."

"And while you're there, ask him to the Fall Festival."

"What?" Beth looked at her friend in surprise.

"What better way to say that you want to go out with him than to invite him to something the whole town is going to?"

"I couldn't do that."

"Yes. You could." Sophie leaned back from the table and grinned again. "And you know, it will drive Dobbs crazy to see you there with Mac. That's a plus."

"I don't think he'd even want to go with me."

"There's only one way to find out."

"Have I ever told you that you're a tough

one to have as a friend? You never let me take the easy way out."

"Just one of the best friend services that I provide."

~

BETH WALKED into Mac's Place and paused, giving her eyes a moment to adjust to the dim lighting. Once again, all the customers were staring at her, the obvious outsider.

The bartender looked up as she approached. He gave her a long glance and tipped his head toward the doorway. "He's upstairs, but I'm warning you, he's in some kind of mood."

Beth nodded and hurried through the doorway. She eyed the stairs, took a deep breath, and started her ascent. Her steps slowed as she got near the top, and she wavered in her decision. Maybe she should just go back downstairs and get back into her car.

No, that was being a coward.

She resolutely climbed the last steps and knocked on his door.

"Come in." Mac's voice didn't sound very welcoming. Not at all.

She opened the door and stepped inside.

Mac froze in place, standing by a table, paper in hand.

"Mac, I've come to…" She took a few steps toward him. "I've come to apologize."

He looked at her in stony silence.

"I'm sorry. I am. I shouldn't have doubted you."

"Apology accepted. Now if you don't mind, I'm very busy." His tone of voice belied any sincerity that he'd actually accepted her apology.

She started to turn and leave. He obviously was in no mood to talk. Then she stopped, turned around, and walked over to stand beside him. "Mac, I *am* sorry. Truly, truly sorry. Of course, you would never slit my tires. I shouldn't have asked you again. You'd already said you hadn't done it. I should have trusted you."

He set the paper he was holding down on the table but still didn't look at her.

She reached out and touched his arm. "I *do* trust you." She found small comfort in the fact he didn't jerk his arm away from her touch.

He turned to look at her now.

"I really do wish you could find a way to forgive me. Maybe we could find a way to start again? I've…" She took a deep breath and looked directly into his eyes. "I don't know when it happened exactly, but I've come to... care about you. I consider you a friend. I do. And I treated you badly. I'm so sorry."

He slowly reached out and turned her to face him, one strong hand on each of her shoulders. "Listen closely. I do *not* want to be your friend."

CHAPTER 16

Mac searched Beth's face, his heart pounding and his pulse racing through his veins like a wild mustang set free in a meadow.

"Mac—"

He put one finger against her lips. Her very soft lips. "I don't want to be just your friend. I want more."

Her eyes widened.

"I also very badly want to kiss you right now." He rubbed his thumb along her lips. "Do you think that's a good idea?"

"I—" She nodded slowly. "I do."

He slowly lowered his lips to cover hers, and a bolt of electricity shot through him. He wrapped his arms around her and pulled her closer. She fit perfectly against him, like the last piece in a jigsaw puzzle. A small sigh escaped her lips, and he was pretty sure it was his undoing. He deepened the kiss, then slowly, ever so slowly pulled away from her delicious lips but kept her in his arms. "I've been wanting to do that since the last time."

"The last time?"

"When we were kids."

"You remember that?"

"Oh yes, I remember it. That kiss has haunted me all these years." He brushed the back of his hand along the silken softness of her cheek. "I didn't know if you'd remember it, though."

"I do remember it." She looked up at him. "So, does this mean you've forgiven me?"

"Woman, I'm fairly certain that I'd do anything you want, including accepting your apology. There might be a small price to pay, though."

"What's that?"

"Another kiss." He leaned down and kissed her again.

~

BETH LAUGHED as Mac pulled away from her lips the second time. "I think that's a fair price to pay." She reached up and touched his face, rough with a day's growth of beard. "In fact, if you asked me to pay again, I wouldn't argue."

He threw back his head in a marvelous, deep chuckle. "I'll have to see about collecting again then."

He took her hand in his and led her over to the couch where she wasn't embarrassed to admit they made out for a while like a couple of teenagers. Her lips were warm and her face slightly heated from the scrape of his whiskers against her cheeks.

He trailed a finger along her jawline. "If I'd known that was going to happen, I would have shaved before you came over."

"My fault for surprising you."

"I'll say this has been a surprise." He tucked her against his side.

She relaxed against him, savoring just leaning against him.

"So, how about I take you out on a real date tonight? Like for a real meal. We could go to Antonio's. It's still open, isn't it?"

"I can't."

She felt him tense against her. "I've asked you out a few times now. I'm beginning to think you really don't want to be seen with me, do you?"

"It's not that. I mean I can't tonight. I have plans with Sophie." She knew that Sophie would be totally fine if she canceled, but she needed some time to figure this all out. All of a sudden her life had turned upside down. And not in a bad way, just a different sort of way.

"Okay." He didn't sound convinced.

She didn't want him to think that she didn't want to be seen with him. Though, to be honest, at first she *hadn't* wanted to be seen with him. *How shallow was that?* Not one of her finer moments. She needed to make things right with him. "How about you come to the Fall Festival with me this weekend?"

He cocked his head to the side. "Really? Are you sure? The whole town is going to be there. There'll be talk. Beth Cassidy with Mac McKenna."

"I *am* sure."

He smiled at her then, a smile that said he was pleased, he was happy. A smile that promised that they'd see what the future had in store for them.

"I think I should pay the price again." She squeezed his hand, then leaned over and kissed him yet again.

CHAPTER 17

"Y ou guys all ready to go?" Nora walked into Beth's kitchen on Saturday.

"Almost, Grams." Trevor hugged her. "I can't find my shoes."

"You can't ever find your shoes." Connor rolled his eyes and let out an exaggerated sigh. "C'mon. Let's go find them. The sooner we do, the sooner we can go to the Fall Festival."

The boys raced out of the room and she turned to Beth. She paused and stared at her daughter for a moment. "Is everything okay?"

"Of course." Beth's words came out a bit too rushed.

"You looked flushed… and that outfit." She'd expected Beth to be dressed in jeans and a flannel shirt, or possibly a sweater. Beth was wearing nice corduroy slacks and a pretty top that she hadn't seen before.

"What's wrong with it?" Beth glanced down and frowned.

"I was just expecting something more..." Nora shook her head. "Never mind, you look very lovely."

"Well, I am running for mayor and most of the town will be there. I wanted to look nice."

She couldn't put her finger on it, but something was going on with her daughter. She seemed edgy. Or maybe a bit exhilarated? Nora hadn't seen Beth this excited about going to the Fall Festival since she'd been a young girl.

She followed Beth out of the kitchen and into the family room. Beth glanced at her reflection in the mirror hanging over a small table. She fussed with a loose wisp of hair.

Nora frowned. Something was going on, for sure.

"Come on, boys. Let's go." Beth called out then turned to Nora. "Oh, and I'm meeting Mac at the festival.

Ah, so that was it. Nora smiled to herself, her faith in her mother's intuition fully intact. Her daughter's nonchalant tone of voice hadn't fooled her for a moment. Well, good for Beth.

She made a mental note to take the boys off her daughter's hands when they got to the festival. She figured offering to take them on some of the rides would work. She herded the boys out to her car, and they all headed to the festival.

She couldn't help but smile when she saw Beth flip down the sun visor and take a quick look in the mirror on the back side of it, fussing with an imaginary fly-away wisp yet again.

Well, well, well.

BETH STOOD at the edge of the crowd at the Fall Festival after her mother took the boys off to have fun on the rides. She should have set up a place to meet Mac instead of just saying she'd see him here. Main Street was teeming with people milling about and ducking in and out of the shops. The park at the end of the street held a few rides. Vendors were set up along Main Street and the road had been closed to car traffic. She took out her phone and texted Mac that she'd be waiting in front of Bookish Cafe, she'd never find him if they didn't set a meeting place.

She wandered along the street, stopping to talk to people along the way. She quit counting how many times she'd glanced at her phone to see if Mac had answered her text.

Maybe he'd decided not to come or got busy at the tavern.

She could see all the way down the sidewalk to Annie's shop, and Mac wasn't waiting for her there. Disappointment hovered around her.

She shoved her phone back into her pocket. She was going to enjoy herself anyway. *She was.*

She continued down the street and stopped at Annie's shop. Annie stood in the doorway, welcoming people to Bookish Cafe. "Hi, Beth."

"Hey, Annie. Looks like you have a good crowd at your shop today."

"We're doing a brisk business. I even put Nick to work at the checkout counter. Is your mom around?"

"She took the boys over to the rides."

"You want to come in and grab a coffee or soda?"

"I… uh… I'm meeting someone here."

One of Annie's eyebrows cocked questioningly. "Oh?"

"I'm meeting Mac McKenna."

Annie didn't look surprised. "I haven't seen him."

"Yet here I am."

Beth turned at the sound of Mac's voice. He greeted her with a warm smile. She felt a smile spread across her face. Maybe even a goofy smile. She was just so glad to see him. She was uncertain on whether she should give him a quick hug or what. They both stood awkwardly in front of Annie.

"Well, go on you two. Go have fun. If you see your mom, tell her to stop by with the boys and I'll get them some ice cream." Annie shooed them down the street.

Beth fell into step beside Mac as they threaded through the crowd. They almost got separated when a large group passed by walking in the opposite direction. He grabbed her hand to keep from losing her, then kept her hand in his as they ambled along the sidewalk in a less crowded area.

She enjoyed the feeling of her hand in his strong grip. It had been years and years since she'd walked hand in hand with a man. They wandered over to the large bricked courtyard area that led to the river walk.

"Well, Miss Cassidy." Mr. Dobbs stood in the middle of the path, blocking their way.

"Mr. Dobbs." Beth forced a smile. She was having too good of a time with Mac to deal with Dobbs today. She started to sidestep him.

"So, you're here with Mac McKenna?" He eyed her and shook his head with obvious disapproval.

"I am." She moved closer to Mac and squeezed his hand.

"Hm. Well, that's interesting."

"Say, *darlin'*, you want to go walk along the river?" Mac wrapped his arm around her shoulder and pulled her close.

Dobbs' eyes widened.

She knew that Mac was just trying to get a rise out of Dobbs with the darling remark and the easy draping of his arm around her shoulder. She didn't blame him. Dobbs seemed to bring out the... well, she didn't know what to call it exactly, but he sure rubbed her the wrong way with his judgmental attitude.

Dobbs shook his head again, turned away without another word, and hurried over to where James Weaver stood on the far side of the courtyard. He leaned over and said something to James and they both stared over at her and Mac.

"Come on. Let's do go walk along the river." She tugged on Mac's hand and they headed to the path along Sweet River.

"Sorry, Old Man Dobbs just gets to me." Mac sighed.

"He gets under my skin, too."

"I'm not sure I'm doing your campaign for mayor any favors."

"I don't know what you mean." But she did. Mac had a reputation and so far the town had yet to forget it.

"I wonder if this is very smart. Wandering around town with me." He looked down at their hands then held them up. "Like this."

"Mac, there is nowhere I'd rather be right now and no one I'd rather be with." She squeezed his hand.

MAC LIKED the feel of Beth's hand in his. He liked the feel of her walking beside him. And he liked that she hadn't pulled away from him when Dobbs showed up. Oh, heck, he liked *everything*

about this day so far. His life had been totally turned upside down since that day he'd stopped by the side of the road to help her. He thanked his lucky stars, the fates, and anyone else who needed thanking for that pivotal day and what he now considered her serendipitous flat tire.

He felt a foolish grin spread across his face as they headed across the courtyard.

"Mom! Mom." Trevor called from across the courtyard and waved his arm excitedly.

Beth slipped her hand from his as Trevor raced across the bricks with Connor and Nora trailing behind. Mac glanced down at his empty hand, momentarily disconnected from Beth and his thoughts.

"Sorry, I…" she whispered to him as Trevor got closer.

He nodded. He understood. Kind of. She wasn't ready for the boys to know he was more than just an acquaintance, a friend.

Was he more than that?

Of course, he was…

"Hey, Mr. McKenna. You're here too. Isn't the festival the best? Grams took us on the rides."

"Hey, Trev. Good to see you."

Connor and Nora walked up. Nora flashed

him a welcoming smile. "Good to see you, Mac. Enjoying the festival?"

"I am. I haven't been to it since high school days." The last time he'd been to one, he'd sat at the edge of town and watched the people milling around. Friends laughing and joking together. Families out for a day of fun. He'd been all alone and unnoticed. He'd finally left when he couldn't bear the weight of the ache of loneliness. Until rescuing Beth by the side of the road, he hadn't been back to Sweet River Falls since he'd moved away from its judgmental people like Old Man Dobbs.

"Mom, Annie said you should bring the boys by Bookish Cafe and get some ice cream."

"Can we?" Connor looked at Nora.

"Of course." She turned to Beth. "I'll take them to Annie's and we'll meet up there afterward. About thirty minutes or so? Does that sound good?"

"Sure. Thanks, Mom."

Mac watched as Trevor ran ahead of Nora and Connor, then came racing back toward them again. They walked around a bend in the river and disappeared.

Mac wasn't used to being around kids, but he enjoyed Beth's boys. He'd had a good time helping them with their tree house. He just hadn't realized the energy level of boys that age. "He's got a lot of energy."

"No kidding." Beth grinned and slipped her hand back into his. "I'm sorry about the hand thing. The boys. I'm not sure I'm ready for them to know I'm…" She looked at him. "What am I? Seeing you? Dating you?"

"I don't know what people call this. Don't care." He softly tucked a wisp of her hair away from her face. "I like you, Beth Cassidy."

A shy grin crossed her face. "I like you, Mac McKenna."

They came up to Brooks Gallery and Beth grabbed his hand. "Come on. Let's go in and say hi to Sophie."

"Does she work at her parents' gallery now?" He remembered they'd owned the artsy-craftsy gallery.

Beth stopped and looked at him, a sad look crossing her face. "Her parents died in a car accident. Sophie was teaching music at the high school, but after they died she took over the gallery."

"That's too bad. About her parents, I mean."

"She loved teaching, but I think she felt… I

don't know… obligated to take over the gallery. Her parents had worked so hard to get it up and running and successful. Anyway, she makes some jewelry for the shop. She's always been so creative. Then she buys local crafts and photography." She tugged on his hand. "Come in and see for yourself."

They walked through the open door, and Sophie waved at them. They wandered around the gallery while Sophie finished up with her customers and came up to them. "Hey, you two."

"I wanted to show Mac your gallery."

"It's really nice. I love those black and white photos over there of the mountains. And that one of the tree fallen across the river. The lighting in it is spectacular."

"And you, Mac McKenna, have a good eye." Sophie smiled at him. "Those were taken by a very talented photographer, Hunt Robichaux. I'm trying to arrange a whole showing for him here at the gallery of his Rocky Mountain photography."

"Beth said you make some of the jewelry here. Did you make the silver set with the denim turquoise?"

"I did." Sophie beamed. "And you know your stones."

"It's great work." Mac had been impressed with the symmetry and craftsmanship of the set.

"Okay, Beth, you can bring this man back here any time you want." Sophie grinned. "Oh, gotta run. More customers. I'll catch you later. Thanks for stopping by."

Sophie leaned over and whispered something to Beth, too low for him to catch any of the words. Beth blushed a delightful shade of rosy pink.

"What was that all about?" He cocked his head to the side.

"Just… Sophie being Sophie."

They walked back out into the sunshine. They continued down the river walk, back in the direction of Bookish Cafe. He felt her shiver and looked down at her. "You cold?"

"The temperature has dropped a bit, hasn't it? I guess I should have worn a sweater."

"I've got a jeans jacket in my truck. Let me run and get it. Won't take but a few minutes. It will be a tad large on you, but at least you won't be cold."

"Okay. I am chilly. I'll meet you back by

Annie's and we'll walk around that end of town until Mom and the boys are ready."

"I'll be right back."

He hurried down the pathway, back out to the street, and over to the parking area. The lot was full of cars now, and for a minute or so he couldn't figure out where he'd parked his truck. He wandered around the area until he found it, making a mental note where it was so he could find it again when it was time to leave.

He snatched the jacket from the car and headed back toward Bookish Cafe. Just as he got close, Daniel Smith stepped in front of him. "Mr. McKenna, I need a word with you."

He gritted his teeth. Danny Boy was getting on his last nerve. "What?" He saw Beth approaching them with a questioning look on her face.

"Some cars were broken into at the parking lot. You were seen walking around the lot."

"So were a million other people."

Beth walked up to his side. "What's going on?"

Before she could get her answer, the boys and Nora came out of Bookish Cafe. Great, he could have a full audience while he was questioned.

"Hey, Mr. McKenna. You should have had ice cream with us." Trevor came up beside him and tugged on his arm. "I had chocolate."

"Daniel?" Beth asked again.

"I was just telling Mr. McKenna that some cars were broken into in the parking area."

"Oh, did someone break into his truck?"

"No, Mr. McKenna was seen walking through the parking lot, though."

Beth reached out and took the jacket from him. "He was getting this for me. I was cold." She shrugged into the jacket as if to prove her point. "So you were wondering if he saw anyone suspicious while he was getting this for me?"

"No, I was actually questioning him regarding the break-ins. He does always seem to be around when there's trouble. Awfully convenient coincidence, don't you think?"

"Mr. McKenna wouldn't break anything." Trevor stood in front of him and faced off with the officer.

"What's going on?"

Mac looked at the man who walked up to them. He looked vaguely familiar.

"Dad." Trevor raced over and threw himself into the man's arms.

CHAPTER 18

"Scott, what are you doing here?" Beth looked at her ex-husband. In typical Scott fashion, he hadn't mentioned he was coming to the festival. She actually thought he was still out of the country on business.

"Got back earlier than I thought from my trip. Thought I'd come by and see the boys." Scott reached out his hand. "Daniel, good to see you."

Daniel shook his hand.

"What's going on? Is there a problem?" Scott eyed all of them.

"Just asking Mr. McKenna a few questions."

"Mr. McKenna is my friend. He didn't break any cars." Trevor stepped over in front of Mac and slipped his hand in Mac's.

Scott narrowed his eyes. "Mac McKenna? I remember you from school days."

Beth saw the look. He remembered Mac as the kid with the troublemaker reputation.

"Some cars were broken into at the parking area. Mr. McKenna was seen in the area. He was also seen at the site when your wife's tire was slashed."

"I'm not his wife." Beth corrected. "And Mac wasn't involved in the tire incident."

"He also had access to her keys when her house was broken into."

"What? The house was broken into?" Scott shot her an accusing look. "Don't you think that was something to tell me since my sons live there?"

"I was going to tell you when you got back from your trip. It's not like you could have done anything while you were in Europe. I handled it."

And it wasn't like he'd called the boys during the weeks and weeks he'd been away, either.

"Can we not talk about this here? Now?" She looked pointedly at the boys.

"I think I'm going to take the boys back for some more rides. What do you say?" her mom offered.

"No, I want to take them for ice cream." Scott stopped her.

"We just had ice cream, Dad," Connor said.

Scott looked incredibly annoyed. "I only have a few minutes. I thought I could at least take my sons for ice cream."

"I didn't know you were coming, Scott." Beth pointed out the obvious, annoyed that Scott was annoyed. Annoyed at Daniel Smith. Annoyed that Scott hadn't bothered to say he was coming to the festival.

"We could have *more* ice cream," Trevor suggested.

Scott looked at his watch. "I really need to get home, anyway. Been away a long time. I'll see you boys soon."

Scott walked up to her, leaned close, and put a strong grip on her arm. "I don't want that Mac McKenna anywhere near my sons. He's nothing but trouble."

By the look on Mac's face, it was obvious he'd heard Scott's not so quiet whisper. So had her mother, because her face held a disapproving look. She wasn't Scott's fan even on a good day, though she never let on to the boys.

Beth pulled her arm from Scott's grasp. "We'll talk later."

"Bye, boys." Scott turned away and stalked off down the sidewalk without so much as a hug for the boys or a civil goodbye to her mom.

"We're going to go on just a few more rides, how about that?" Nora looked directly at her, her eyes filled with support.

"Yes, that's fine. I'll meet you here in a bit."

She watched as her mom led the boys away then turned to Daniel, still standing beside them. "So, you're finished, right?"

He looked at Mac, then back to her. "For now." He turned and headed down the sidewalk.

"Mac, I'm so sorry. Sorry about all of this."

"NONE OF THIS IS YOUR FAULT." Mac raked his hand through his hair.

"I'm still sorry." She rested her hand on his arm. The sleeve of the jeans jacket almost covered her hand.

"I can't seem to shake my prior reputation."

"If people would just take some time to get to know you now." She shook her head.

"Anyway, I don't think your reputation was deserved back then. I don't think anyone gave you a chance."

"Appears they still don't want to." He took her hand and led her over to a bench. "I think we should talk."

"Okay." Beth slipped down onto the bench, and he refused to think about how adorable she looked in his jeans jacket.

"I…" He didn't know how to even say the words that he really didn't want to say. But they needed to be said.

"What?" She looked up at him, her eyes trusting and full of support.

He was going to ruin that. Ruin everything. But it was for the best.

"I don't think this is working out."

"What's not?" Her eyes clouded with worry.

"Your whole life is here in this town. The boys, your family, your job. You're even running for mayor of the town."

"And?"

"And this town is never going to change. They aren't going to change their opinion of me or give me a chance. They'll always think the worst of me."

"Just give it some time." She reached out and took his hands in hers.

He ignored how soft they were, how warm.

"Beth, I do care about you. My time with you has been special. But I don't think we should continue seeing each other."

"Yes, we should."

"No, we shouldn't. I… I *can't*." He took his hands away from her grasp. "I can't keep coming back here and be questioned by the police for every little thing that happens here. I've worked really hard to get to where I am now. A business owner where people like me and respect me. It took me years to have any confidence in myself. I can't let this town destroy me."

"Mac, don't do this. We'll work it out."

He reached out and touched her face. "I have to. This town will destroy me, but it's woven all through your life. I'll ruin your chance at being elected mayor, and you heard your ex. He doesn't want me around the boys. I don't want to cause problems for you and him and the boys."

"I don't care about that. Scott doesn't control my life. And if being with you costs me the mayor job, I don't care about that either."

"I care." He slowly took his hand away from her face. "This is for the best. For you. For me. I can't let this town destroy me."

"Mac, please. Let's work this out." Her eyes pleaded with him and tore a hole the size of Montana in his heart.

"I've got to go." He stood up.

She stared at him with the saddest eyes he'd ever seen. "Your jacket." Her voice was barely a whisper as she started to shrug out of the jacket.

"Keep it."

He turned away and strode down the sidewalk before those sad eyes made him change his mind. He was doing the right thing. For both of them.

But if it was so right, why could he barely breathe? Why was there such an ache oozing through every fiber of his body?

"Goodbye, Beth." He whispered the words into the cool Colorado breeze and they drifted off into eternity.

CHAPTER 19

The heat of a lone tear trailed down Beth's cheek. She swiped at it with the palm of her hand. She watched as Mac walked away until she could no longer see him. She kept herself from racing after him and throwing herself into his arms because part of what he'd said was right.

She didn't care about Scott's threats or how being seen with Mac might affect her running for mayor. Not a bit. But she understood how Sweet River Falls was crushing Mac's soul. He'd tried too hard to outrun his reputation. He finally fit in at Mac's Place in Mountain Grove. The people there liked him and trusted him. He wasn't being questioned by the police at every turn.

And he was right about another thing. Her life was entwined with Sweet River Falls. Her family and her job. Everything was here.

Sometimes the fates were cruel. They brought someone special into your life but then took them away, leaving a gaping hole in your heart.

"You okay?" Her mother stood at the end of the bench, her eyes filled with concern.

"Where are the boys?" She avoided her mother's question.

"Right over there. See? They're watching Jimmy Nelson at the face painting booth." Nora sat beside her. "Now, tell me what's wrong."

Her mother wasn't one to let things go. Beth turned to her and tried to put on a smile. "Oh, Mac and I decided not to see each other anymore."

"Why in the world would you do that? I've seen how you look at him. You care about him."

"I do. But… well, it's complicated. It just wasn't… right… for us."

"I don't believe that for a second." Nora narrowed her eyes. "Did you just get scared? It is hard to trust again after what Scott did, but honey, you have to take chances in life. If you don't, you miss so much."

"It was a bit scary, but it wasn't that. It just… it wasn't working for us."

Her mother didn't look convinced but dropped the topic when the boys hurried up to them.

"Where's Mr. McKenna?" Trevor peered around the crowd.

"He had to go home."

"That's too bad. I wanted to see if he'd come over and play in our tree house again." Trevor frowned.

"I think it's time we head out, boys." Nora stood.

"Already?" Connor scowled.

"We've been here for hours. Let's head out. How would you boys like to stay with me tonight?"

"Yes." Trevor fist pumped the air.

"Beth, you want to come stay too?"

"No, I think I'll just have you drop me off at home."

Her mother didn't look happy at that decision but nodded. The four of them wound their way through the crowd to the parking area. She glanced back one more time, looking at the bench where she'd been sitting. Where Mac had touched her face. Her heart crumbling with the thought that it was the last time she'd ever feel his hand on her. She grabbed the edges of his jacket and wrapped it tightly against her body as if his very arms were around her.

BETH CHANGED into her favorite flannel pajamas after her mother dropped her off. She wandered aimlessly around the house, picking up toys, stacking magazines. The pile of papers to grade beckoned her, but she couldn't convince herself to sit down and work on them.

She slipped Mac's jacket on over her pjs and went out to sit on her back porch. She sat sipping a glass of wine and watching as the evening darkened, surrounding her in its shadowy cloak.

She hadn't felt this lonely in… well, she'd never felt this lonely before. She hadn't even felt this deserted when Scott had left her. Now she felt like she was being swept down the river, adrift, with no way to catch hold and get back under control.

She swiped at yet another tear. She wasn't usually a crying person, but the ache inside of her just would not abate.

"There you are." Sophie came walking around the side of the house. "I saw your car and knocked, but you didn't answer. Figured you were back here."

Beth took one look at Sophie and burst into tears. Sophie, her best friend, the one who always seemed to know when she needed her. She let the tears flow freely now, and Sophie sat down beside her and wrapped her in her arms.

Sophie let her cry it out, then sat back and looked at her. "So, what happened?"

"It's Mac."

"You two looked cozy when you came by the gallery. What happened?"

"Everything fell apart."

"I'm going to need more than that…" Sophie jumped up. "Just a sec. I'm going to go grab a glass of wine for me."

Sophie came back with a glass of wine and an afghan. She settled beside Beth and pulled the afghan around them to chase off the chill of the evening. "Okay, now tell me what happened."

"Let's see. There was Daniel Smith confronting Mac about break-ins to the cars in the parking lot."

"Why would he question Mac?"

"Because Mac was seen walking through the lot."

"I'd imagine hundreds of other people were too."

"Well, I think Daniel is convinced that Mac is behind a bunch of problems in town."

Sophie took a sip of her wine and a thoughtful look crossed her face. "I think Daniel still has a crush on you and he's jealous of Mac."

"What?" She shook her head. "No, that's crazy."

"Is it?" Sophie eyed her.

"I don't know…" Beth thought about it. She'd known that Daniel had had a crush on her in high school and maybe even still did? All these years later? "Maybe…"

"Maybe, nothing. I bet that's why he's got such a target on Mac."

"Well, then it got worse."

"Worse?"

"Scott showed up."

"I thought he was off somewhere in Europe."

"Well, he's back. The boys were there, Daniel was there accusing Mac of the break-ins, puncturing my tire, and mentioned he'd had access to my keys before the house got broken into." Beth let out a long sigh. "Scott got mad I hadn't told him about the house being broken into, but I had every intention of telling him after he got back into the country. Then he demanded that I keep Mac away from the boys. Said Mac was a bad influence."

"He can't tell you what to do like that."

"Evidently he thinks he can. And Mac heard him say it to me."

Sophie scowled. "Scott likes to blow into town, tell you what to do, then just drop out of sight for months on end."

She sniffled and snatched a tissue from her pocket, done with this crying jag. "Anyway, after Daniel left and Scott stalked off, Mom took the boys to ride a few more rides." She tugged the afghan closer, tucking her feet beneath her. "Mac said we should talk… and he said we should stop seeing each other."

"Because of what Scott said?"

"Partly. But also because he just can't be pushed back into trying to defend himself all the time. So many people in Sweet River Falls just look at him as the troublemaker. They aren't willing to give him a chance. I think it took years for him to overcome his insecurities from growing up here and always being an outsider.

He fits in over in Mountain Grove. He doesn't want to be constantly questioned and reminded of his past. I can't blame him."

"And your life is here in Sweet River Falls."

"My life, my family, my job." Beth took a sip of her wine. "Not to mention I'm running for mayor. He thinks being seen with him will hurt my chances of getting elected."

"It does get complicated."

"I just… I *like* him. I like him a lot. I finally admitted it to myself and to Mac."

"Don't you think you two could work it out?"

"I don't think it's fair to Mac to even ask that. He can't stand coming to Sweet River Falls, and I don't blame him. I'm sure it brings up memories of everything that he's tried to put behind him. And how would that work? I'd only go over to Mountain Grove?"

"I don't know. It just seems like a shame to let it all die before you even got a chance at seeing where it was going. And I'm telling you, it was going somewhere. I saw him looking at you when you were at the gallery. He's smitten."

"I think we just found each other at the wrong time in our lives." She sat quietly beside her friend as they gazed up at the stars blinking across the night sky. Just having Sophie here with her was enough to soothe her jangled nerves.

She turned to Sophie. "You're always here for me. I don't know what I'd do without you."

Sophie smiled. "You'll never have to find out. We're a team. Best friends for life."

CHAPTER 20

Mac had sworn he'd never set foot in Sweet River Falls again, but he also was not going to disappoint Jimmy Nelson. He was going to drop off some books for him at the school, with a note to his mother saying he'd be glad to continue with Jimmy if she'd drive him over to Mountain Grove. Then he'd scuff the dust of Sweet River Falls off his boots and be done with it. Done with everyone in the town. Done with their judgmental attitude.

He just prayed he wouldn't run into Beth at the school because he didn't want his resolve to waver. He knew he'd made the right decision, both for Beth and for him. He and Beth were just not meant to be. Star-crossed lovers—not that they were *lovers*. But he did care for her.

He'd been miserable since they'd talked last weekend. He'd slammed around his apartment and done every job he'd been avoiding doing at the tavern. Anything and everything to keep mindlessly busy.

He pulled into the parking lot of the school and gritted his teeth. He could do this. A quick in and out.

Yet, he sat there staring at the school, his feet unwilling to carry him inside. He glanced down to the far end of the school and squinted against the glare.

Was that...

Smoke. That *was* smoke.

He flung open the door to the truck and hurled himself across the parking lot. He grabbed the first door he came to, but it was locked. Of course. Things change. Schools don't leave all the doors open.

He whirled around and ran to the front door, slamming through it, and spied the fire alarm on the wall. He tripped the alarm and without skipping a beat raced down the hallway.

Teachers began to usher the students outside. He sped around the corner to the L-shaped hallway at the end of the school. A group of kids came out of the smoky hallway with a teacher leading the way. She looked at him, her eyes filled with worry. "I've got these kids, but Miss Jesse is still back there. Some kids were still in the art room. It's really not more than a closet off of our class. Then flames jumped across the hallway and I saw her take them back into the room."

"Get these kids to safety. I'll go get her and the other kids."

He looked at the flames shooting across the floor. He stripped off his shirt and soaked it in the water fountain and splashed water down his jeans. It would have to do. With a running start, he raced down the hall, pressing the wet shirt to his face, and leaped over the flames.

"Over here." A teacher called out to him through a slightly opened door.

He hurried the rest of the way to her class, tears streaming down his face, and slipped through her door. The flames rapidly approached behind him.

The teacher had four kids along the back wall, low to the ground. "Flames are blocking our way out."

He looked over at the kids with their wide eyes. Trevor looked back at him with trusting eyes, as if he was here to save the day. Only he didn't know if he could make things happen quick enough. He looked around the room and assessed the situation. "Okay, we'll get them out the windows."

"It's too far too the ground. And the windows aren't made to open since we're up so high."

He crossed over and looked down. The ground sloped away from the building at this side, a good fifteen feet down. It was their only choice. He looked at the ground and outside. No sign of the fire trucks yet. He couldn't even hear sirens.

Trevor was still looking at him with his eyes filled with trust. There was no way he was going to let the boy down. No way. They were going to get out of here.

BETH USHERED her class down the hall single file and out through the door to the playground area. She'd double counted the children, assuring herself that they were all here and safe. When she got the children settled in their assigned location at the far end of the playground, then, and only then, did she scan the playground area, looking for Trevor and Connor. She had to trust that their teachers had done their duty, just like she had, and gotten their students out to safety.

She saw Connor with his class, but when she saw Miss Jesse's assistant teacher, she didn't see Miss Jesse or Trevor. Her heart tripped in her chest. Where were they? She couldn't go over there and ask. She had a responsibility to the children in her class.

Her duty as a teacher and her panic as a mother collided with the force of a tornado. She scanned the area, looking from group to group. No sign of Trevor or Miss Jesse.

Miss Simmons, the assistant principal walked up. "Did you get everyone?" The woman started counting the children sitting on the ground, doing the double check they'd all been taught. "Yes, everyone."

The assistant principal checked off her list.

"Miss Simmons, I don't see Miss Jesse… or Trevor."

"She and some of her students got separated from the rest of the class." Miss Simmons hurried away with her list, doing her job.

But that didn't help the rising panic sweeping through Beth. She looked at the smoke now billowing out of the area of the school that held Trevor's class.

Where was Trevor?

Mac looked around the room. "Get those paint smocks over there and wet them in that sink."

"I'll do it." Trevor jumped up and raced to the sink with a handful of smocks.

"We'll shove some of those under the door to stop the smoke from coming in, and the kids can hold them over their faces. It should help."

He turned to the teacher who was doing an amazing job of staying calm—or pretending to be calm for the kids. "You think you can get the kids into the window and get them to jump to me?"

"But how will we get the window open?"

"I'll break it."

He picked up a desk. "Get the kids back."

She ushered them away from the window. He swung the desk with all his might and smashed it through the glass. He took his shirt and knocked out a few pieces of glass that hung on and wiped away the broken glass from the windowsill.

She nodded and turned to the kids. "We're going out the window. We're going to jump and he's going to catch you. We're all going to be very, very brave."

"I'm Mac." He smiled encouragingly to the kids. "I'm strong enough to catch you, I promise. Keep your faces covered with those wet smocks until it's your turn."

"I'm scared, Miss Jesse." A small girl in a pink dress clung to her teacher. The girl's wide brown eyes were filled with tears.

"It's going to be okay." She assured the girl.

"You got this?" He hated to leave the teacher in here, but didn't know another way. They were running out of time. He took a deep breath to steady his nerves, then coughed. Not the best idea to take deep breaths with the smoky air.

"I've got it." Miss Jesse nodded confidently.

He climbed into the window and lowered himself as far as he could. Then he let go and dropped to the ground below, rolling as he landed. He scrambled to his feet and looked up. "Okay. First one."

The little girl who had been clinging to Miss Jesse appeared in the window. "I can't do it."

Trevor appeared beside her. "I'll go first. Watch me. Mr. McKenna will catch me. Then you do it, too."

The girl nodded.

Trevor maneuvered his way to the window ledge. "I'm jumping now. Watch me. You can do this."

"Okay."

Mac steeled himself and held up his arms. Trevor landed against him and they both fell to the ground with a thud.

Trevor popped up. "I'm good. I knew you'd catch me." He turned and looked up at the window. "Come on, Rita Jo. Jump. It's fine."

"Close your eyes and jump to me, sweetheart. I've got you," Mac called up to the girl.

Miss Jesse pried the girl's hands from the sill and said something to her. The girl screwed up her face with her eyes tightly closed and jumped. He caught her against him and quickly set her down. "Go stand by that tree." He motioned to a tree a safe distance way. "Trevor, go stand by her. You two stay together."

He turned back, and Miss Jesse had another

girl in the window. She jumped to him, and he caught her. The girl hurried over to join her classmates.

He caught the next child, and Miss Jesse poked her head out the window. "Hurry. Smoke is coming in."

She got the last boy into the window and he jumped to Mac. They both tumbled to the ground, but the boy scrambled to his feet. "I'm good. But you have to get Miss Jesse now."

Smoke was rolling out the window around the teacher. "Come on. Jump to me," Mac urged her.

She swung her leg over the sill and lowered herself as far as she could. "I'm letting go, now."

"I've got you."

Miss Jesse landed against him with a thump, and they rolled down the hill. "You okay?" He looked at her closely.

"I think so." She started to push up and a look of pain flashed across her face. "Guess I hurt my ankle. Can you help me up?"

He got to his feet and deftly pulled her up. She leaned against him. "We need to get the kids to our assigned spot so they know we're all okay."

He helped Miss Jesse limp over to the waiting children. "Okay, kids. See, we all made it."

"Miss Jesse, are you hurt?" Trevor looked at his teacher.

"I'll be okay. Just twisted my ankle a bit. I'm afraid I was a bit heavier than you kids." She smiled encouragingly at them. "Let's all hold hands now. We're going to go meet up with the rest of your class."

The one little girl in the pink dress was sitting on the ground quietly sobbing. Mac walked over and reached a hand down. "Come on, sweetheart. It's going to be okay."

"I want my mom."

"I bet you do. Let's go with Miss Jesse, and then I bet your Mom will be able to find you."

He kept one arm around Miss Jesse and led the children away from the building. They walked to their designated spot on the far end of the playground, away from the buildings. He settled Miss Jesse onto the edge of a merry-go-round. A woman came running up to them. "Four?"

"Yes, it's all of them." Miss Jesse coughed.

The woman looked visibly relieved as she

checked off her list. "Everyone out safely and accounted for."

"There was a lot of smoke in the room. I think you should get the EMTs to check out the kids, and Miss Jesse here has something wrong with her ankle."

"You are?" The woman stood looking at him with a confused expression.

Daniel Smith rushed up to them. "Got them all yet?"

"All accounted for, yes."

"That's a relief."

He turned and stared at Mac, his eyes narrowing. "What are you doing here?"

Trevor walked up and slipped his hand in Mac's. "He rescued us."

Miss Jesse nodded and got unsteadily to her feet. "He got us all out."

Mac looked down and saw blood running down his side. He must have cut himself on the glass. He looked around for something to press against the cut, but he'd long since lost his shirt in the chaos.

"So, here you are in the middle of trouble again." Daniel Smith eyed him suspiciously.

"You're darn lucky I got here when I did

and tripped the fire alarm." Mac had had enough of Danny Boy's nonsense.

"Looks like the fire started in the boy's bathroom."

Mac swallowed, fearing what was coming.

"It's not like you haven't started a fire before. Started one in the boys' bathroom if I remember correctly."

Mac stood silently.

"He didn't start the fire, he saved us. He's a hero," Trevor insisted.

"Or he started the fire, then got you all out so he could *look* like a hero." Daniel stood directly in front of his path, blocking his way, preventing him from escaping.

And he needed to escape. He'd gotten the kids out, gotten Trevor out. That's what was important.

"I think I'm going to run you in for questioning. This is too many coincidences in my book. Way too many."

"Mom."

Mac felt Trevor's hand slip out of his and turned to see Beth standing there. Trevor threw himself into this mother's arms.

"Mr. McKenna saved us. All of us. We jumped from the window and it was way, way up high. I jumped first to show the other kids that it would be okay. Only Miss Jesse is bigger than us and she hurt her foot."

Beth brushed a lock of Trevor's hair from his face and scanned him from head to toe. She turned to Mac, her brown eyes overflowing with gratitude. "Thank you, Mac." Her voice wavered as she said the words.

She hugged Trevor tightly. "My class is on the bus and headed to the high school. The parents are supposed to pick up the kids there."

"I think we should get the EMTs over to check the kids out. There was quite a bit of smoke coming into the room." Miss Jesse stood wobbling on one leg.

"Daniel, can you get them over here?" Beth turned to the officer.

"I was getting ready to take Mr. McKenna into the station."

"For saving the kids?" She looked from Daniel and back to Mac, then frowned. "Mac, you're bleeding."

"It's not bad."

"You should get that looked at, too." She swirled back and glared at Daniel. "Now why were you taking Mac in?"

"Well, the fire started in the boys' bathroom. He's done that before."

"Daniel Smith, I'm tired of this ridiculous crusade against Mac. I'll be forever grateful that he got Trevor and the other kids out safely. Unless you have proof and you're pressing charges, I'm going to get Mac some help and see that he's checked out."

"If anything at all points at him, I'm heading over to Mountain Grove and arresting him." Daniel turned and walked away.

Beth looked at him. "I'm going to get the EMTs."

"Have them check out the kids and Miss Jesse. I'm fine." He glanced down at the slice on his side. He'd had worse.

"I think you should have that looked at."

"No."

"Mac, I—"

"Beth, there's nothing more to say. I am *so* done with Sweet River Falls."

He turned away and headed back to his truck.

Now, *now* he was finished with this town.

Forever.

And he meant it this time.

CHAPTER 21

Beth sat in Sophie's apartment the next evening after their yoga class. "It was terrible, Soph. Terrible. Here Mac had just saved Trevor and the other kids and Miss Jesse, and there was Daniel, accusing him of starting the fire." Beth shuddered. "I can barely stand to think about Trevor locked in that room with the fire approaching. Mac was the one who saw the smoke and pulled the fire alarm. He gave all of us more time to get out safely. What if Mac wouldn't have happened by the school then?"

"But he was there." Sophie placed her hand over Beth's. "He got everyone out."

"And he was repaid for his heroism by being accused by Daniel Smith of starting the fire."

Beth shook her head. "Mac's right. He's never going to outrun his reputation in this town."

"Or, you could go confront Daniel." Sophie jumped up. "Yes, that's what you should do. Go talk to him. Call him out. Point out why he's being such a jerk."

"I can't do that. What do I say? Hey, I know you've had a crush on me since high school?"

"Yes, you do exactly that." Sophie reached down and tugged her to her feet. "Go now. Talk to him."

"But—"

"Listen, it's up to you to try and make things right with Mac. Or… you can let him go without a fight. Your choice. But don't come moping around me because you didn't try everything to make things work."

Beth stared at Sophie. She was right. Very right. She could let Mac go and then, what? Live without him in her life? The very thought of it was soul-crushing. She wanted him in her life. All the time. Every day.

Beth snatched up her purse. "I'm going to the police station right now."

"You go, girl." Sophie grinned.

Beth hurried out of the apartment and down the sidewalk until she reached the police station. She pushed through the door, her shoulders set in determination.

Daniel looked up from his desk. "Beth." He stood up clumsily and spilled a pile of papers on the floor. "What are you doing here?"

"I need to talk to you. Ask you a question."

"Sure. What?"

She crossed over to stand right beside him. "Do you have a crush on me?"

His face went white, then flushed to a bright red. "What?"

"A crush. A thing. Do you like me?"

"I… uh…"

"I've thought since high school that you've had this little crush thing on me."

"I… well… maybe. A little."

"Ah, ha. I knew it." She tapped her finger against his chest. "And do you think that little crush is getting in the way of your perspective when it comes to Mac McKenna?"

"What? No, of course not." But his face didn't look very convincing.

She cocked her head and stared at him.

"No, I mean. That wouldn't be very professional of me." He sunk into his chair. "Ah, Beth. No, surely I didn't do that."

She sat in the chair beside him. "And yet, I think you did. Even if you didn't mean to."

"I… I don't know what to say. I'm embarrassed. I shouldn't let my personal feelings get in the way of my professional duties."

"No, you shouldn't." Beth stood up. "I've always considered you a *friend*. Nothing more. But a friend. Friends don't do this."

"Beth, I'm sorry."

"It's not me that you owe the apology to." She walked out of the station and into the refreshing night air. She was going to make this right. She was.

Mac looked up and gritted his teeth when he saw Daniel Smith standing across the bar from him. He had thought that part of his life was over and done. Had they come up with some trumped-up evidence that he was involved in the fire?

"What do you want?" Mac stood and swung a crate of clean glasses onto the counter behind the bar.

"I came to talk to you."

"Got nothing to say to you." Mac turned and headed down the bar, aware that Daniel was following along on the other side. Was the man going to arrest him here in his place of business in front of all of his customers? He didn't put anything past Danny Boy.

"I owe you an apology."

Mac stopped dead in his tracks and turned slowly to face Daniel. "You what?"

"I owe you an apology. It appears the fire was started by some sixth-grade boys at the school. One of the boys finally broke down and told his parents. Felt guilty, I guess. Not sure who all else was involved, but I'm sure we'll find out soon enough. Looks like they're involved with the tire slashing and the break-in at Beth's house, too."

Mac just stared at him.

"So you'll accept my apology?"

"Only, you never actually said you were sorry…" Mac turned his back on Daniel.

"Mac, wait."

He stopped.

"I am sorry. I've been a jerk. I knew even before Beth ever so sternly pointed it out to me."

Mac turned back to face Daniel.

"I let personal feelings get in the way of my job. That's unprofessional and unforgivable. I am sorry." He twisted his hat in his hands. "I've sorta had this... I don't know... thing... for Beth for years. I thought maybe after she got over Scott leaving her that *I'd* have a chance with her. Then you swooped into her life and... well, I figured I'd missed my chance with her. But then you kept showing up when there was trouble and... I thought maybe I'd get another chance with her if you were... out of the picture."

Mac stared at the man standing uncomfortably in front of him, shifting from foot to foot. Mac didn't feel obliged to let him off the hook that easily, so he didn't reply.

"I'll say it again. I'm sorry. It shouldn't have taken Beth to point out what a fool I've been. I should have acted professionally and not just jumped to blame you."

Mac leaned down and shifted a crate of glasses from one shelf to another. A crate that didn't really need to be shifted. He stood up straight.

"So, will you accept my apology?" Daniel held out his hand.

"I'll think about it." Mac turned his back on Daniel, without taking his outstretched hand, and stalked away into the back room of the tavern.

CHAPTER 22

Mac was usually a man of his word. He'd promised himself to never set foot on Sweet River Falls soil again. But he couldn't help himself. Today was a big day for Beth. She and James Weaver were set to speak at the courtyard area off Main Street. The town was having yet another one of its festivals, and he knew just the area where he could hang out and not be seen.

He wanted to hear her speech. He wanted her to succeed. He wanted her to have everything she wanted.

And he wanted one more glimpse of her. Just one more. One more memory of her that he could wrap up carefully and take out at times and turn it over and over in his mind.

A bittersweet memory of what could have been.

He cut through the back way into town and walked down a path that led him across a small footbridge over the river. From there he threaded his way to a thicket of trees on the edge of the brick courtyard.

Sophie was up on a temporary platform with a couple of guys with guitars. She was singing a country song. He was surprised by her voice and its throaty, rich tones. The crowd seemed mesmerized listening to her sing. The words of the song taunted him. A song about leaving your hometown and moving on. This town had a way of always pointing out to him what an outsider he was. He thought he'd faced that demon and moved on with his life, but the haunting melody and words washed over him, bringing with them a familiar emptiness and loneliness.

It was time to put this all behind him and move on.

He should never have come. He started to leave as the last sounds of the song drifted away on the crisp Colorado air.

"Hi, I'm Beth Cassidy as you all know." Beth stood on the platform.

His feet refused to move, and he turned back to watch her.

"I'm running for mayor of Sweet River Falls, but you all know that, too." A smattering of clapping swept through the crowd. "But here's the deal. There's a problem…"

The crowd grew silent.

"You see, I've fallen for a man from our town. Well, he used to be from our town. Mac McKenna. I care about him. I care about him a lot. But it seems that many in this town can't forget the kid he was years ago and are unwilling to see the man he is now."

Mac took a step forward to get a better look.

"And if me seeing Mac is a problem for anyone, if that means you don't want to vote for me, then so be it. I'm going to head over to Mountain Grove and ask him to forgive me. Ask him to give Sweet River Falls another try. And I'd truly appreciate it if all of you could welcome him back here and make him feel a part of this great town of ours."

Mac took another step closer, not believing the words he was hearing. His heart pounded, and he struggled to hear her words above the throbbing of his pulse.

"But if it becomes a choice between Mac

and running for mayor, or even if it becomes a choice between Mac and Sweet River Falls... I'm going to choose Mac. If he'll give me a chance."

She turned and looked his direction then, and their eyes locked. She froze in place, then waved to him to come forward. As if pulled by some kind of magnetic field, he slowly crossed toward her. The crowd parted as he wove his way through the townspeople.

She reached down a hand and pulled him up on the platform with her. "So, Mac McKenna, what do you say? Will you give us another chance?"

He looked in her eyes and in that second took the biggest leap of faith he'd ever taken. "I told you before, I'd do anything you ask of me. Anything. Yes, yes we should try again." He leaned down then and kissed those lips of hers that he'd so been missing.

The crowd erupted in claps and cheers. Beth led the way off the platform, her hand firmly placed in his. People stopped them as they walked by, shaking his hand and clapping him on the back, welcoming him back to town.

James Weaver climbed onto the platform

and tapped the mike. "Can I have your attention? Please?"

The crowd quieted down. Beth stood by his side, her hand laced around his arm.

"I have a few things to say myself. First off, I apologize. It appears my son has gotten into some trouble himself. Kids make stupid decisions. He was one of the kids messing with cars and who started that fire at the school. They didn't mean for it to be an actual fire, just some smoke that would interrupt classes, but it got out of hand and it could have been disastrous. He'll be paying the consequences of his actions, and I apologize on his behalf. He'd be here apologizing himself, but he's grounded for the rest of his life, as near as I can figure." A ripple of laughter went through the crowd.

"And Beth, I'm hoping you'll continue to run against me for mayor. A very worthy opponent. And may the best man—or woman—win."

The crowd broke into applause again, and Mac turned to Beth. "What do you say? You still running for mayor?"

She smiled at him. "If you'll be by my side."

"There's nowhere that I'd rather be." He

kissed her quickly. "Now go up on that platform with James and let the town know."

She hugged him and crossed through the crowd. James reached a hand down and helped her up on the platform. They stood side by side while the high school band began to play.

He looked down when he felt a small hand in his. "Trevor."

"Hey, Mr. McKenna." Trevor looked up at him. "You kissed my mom."

"That I did."

"Does that mean she's your girlfriend?"

"I think it does, buddy. You okay with that?"

"Yep." He nodded.

Mac was strangely happy to get the young boy's approval.

"Do I still call you Mr. McKenna if you're my mom's boyfriend?"

"What would you like to call me?"

"Mac?"

"Mac it is."

"Cool. I'm gonna go tell Connor." Trevor raced away through the crowd.

Sophie came to stand beside him. "So, that all worked out nicely, didn't it?"

He grinned at her. "I think so."

"Good timing on showing up here in town

today, but I'm pretty sure Beth was bent on tracking you down. You just made it easier on her."

"I always want to make it easier for her." He meant it. He wanted nothing more than to make Beth Cassidy happy and help her with whatever she needed, including running for mayor of Sweet River Falls.

Beth threaded her way back through the crowd and came up to him, a wide smile on her face. She slipped her arm around his waist and stood close to him. He felt a slow grin spread across his face. He was beginning to like this dating Beth Cassidy gig.

He leaned over and whispered to her, "I've never been happier."

Sophie rolled her eyes. "I heard that. Just kiss her again already. She's happy too. Happier than I've seen her in forever."

"I *am* happy." Beth turned to him and looked up in his eyes with a look so full of... was that love?

He wasn't sure, but he planned on finding out. Because right in that very moment, he knew he was in love with her and planned on spending the rest of his life showing her.

"Hm, Beth?" He reached out and touched

her face, tilted her chin up so she could look directly at him.

"Yes?"

"I've got some news."

"What's that?"

"I do believe that I've fallen in love with you."

An even wider smile crossed her face, and she threw her arms around him. "That works out perfectly because I've fallen in love with you, too."

He kissed her once more for good measure, then held her close against him. Gratefulness poured through him that she'd had that flat tire and he'd been there to rescue her because right now, he was sure she'd rescued him right back and he was perfectly content with his life. Maybe being back in Sweet River Falls wasn't such a bad thing after all.

Dear Reader,

I hope you enjoyed Beth's story. I started writing Beth's story many, many years ago, but never finished it. When I started writing about the town of Sweet River Falls, I knew her story belonged in this series and I finished her book.

Interested in reading more stories in the Sweet River series? See Book Three, A Song to Remember, and all the books in the series at: https://kaycorrell.com/series-info/sweet-river-series/

Thank you and happy reading!

THANK YOU for reading my story. I hope you enjoyed it. Sign up for my newsletter to be updated with information on new releases, promotions, give-aways, and newsletter-only surprises. The signup is at my website, kaycorrell.com.

Reviews help other readers find new books. I always appreciate when my readers take time to leave an honest review.

I love to hear from my readers. Feel free to contact me at authorcontact@kaycorrell.com

COMFORT CROSSING ~ THE SERIES

The Shop on Main - Book One

The Memory Box - Book Two

The Christmas Cottage - A Holiday Novella (Book 2.5)

The Letter - Book Three

The Christmas Scarf - A Holiday Novella (Book 3.5)

The Magnolia Cafe - Book Four

The Unexpected Wedding - Book Five

The Wedding in the Grove (crossover short story between series - Josephine and Paul from The Letter.)

LIGHTHOUSE POINT ~ THE SERIES

Wish Upon a Shell - Book One

Wedding on the Beach - Book Two

Love at the Lighthouse - Book Three

Cottage near the Point - Book Four

Return to the Island - Book Five

Bungalow by the Bay - Book Six

SWEET RIVER ~ THE SERIES

A Dream to Believe in - Book One

A Memory to Cherish - Book Two

A Song to Remember - Book Three

INDIGO BAY ~ a multi-author series of sweet romance

Sweet Sunrise - Book Three

Sweet Holiday Memories - A short holiday story

Sweet Starlight - Book Nine

ABOUT THE AUTHOR

Kay writes sweet, heartwarming stories that are a cross between women's fiction and contemporary romance. She is known for her charming small towns, quirky townsfolk, and enduring strong friendships between the women in her books.

Kay lives in the Midwest of the U.S. and can often be found out and about with her camera, taking a myriad of photographs which she likes to incorporate into her book covers. When not lost in her writing or photography, she can be found spending time with her ever-supportive husband, knitting, or playing with her puppies —two cavaliers and one naughty but adorable Australian shepherd. Kay and her husband also love to travel. When it comes to vacation time, she is torn between a nice trip to the beach or the mountains—but the mountains only get considered in the summer—she swears she's allergic to snow.

Learn more about Kay and her books at kaycorrell.com

While you're there, sign up for her newsletter to hear about new releases, sales, and giveaways.

WHERE TO FIND ME:
kaycorrell.com
authorcontact@kaycorrell.com

Join my Facebook Reader Group. We have lots of fun and you'll hear about sales and new releases first!
https://www.facebook.com/groups/KayCorrell/

 facebook.com/KayCorrellAuthor

 instagram.com/kay5

 pinterest.com/kaycorrellauthor

 amazon.com/author/kaycorrell

 bookbub.com/authors/kay-correll

Made in the USA
Monee, IL
08 September 2021